THE CELEBRATED JUMPING FROG OF CALAVERAS COUNTY

AND OTHER HUMOROUS TALES

First Warbler Press Edition 2022

"The Celebrated Jumping Frog of Calaveras County" first published in 1865 in *The New York Saturday Press* | Private History of the "Jumping Frog" by Mark Twain first appeared in *The North American Review*, Apr., 1894, Vol. 158, No. 449, pp. 446–453. | "Cannibalism in the Cars" first published in 1868 in *The Broadway Annual* | "Journalism in Tennessee" first published in 1869 in the Buffalo *Express* | "How I Edited an Agricultural Paper" first published in 1870 in *Galaxy* | "The Stolen White Elephant" first published in 1882 by James R. Osgood | "The Invalid's Story" first published in 1882 in *The Stolen White Elephant, Etc.* |"Luck" first published in 1891 in *Harper's Magazine* | "Hunting the Deceitful Turkey" first published in 1906 in *Harper's Magazine*

ISBN 978-1-957240-93-0 (paperback)
ISBN 978-1-957240-94-7 (e-book)

warblerpress.com

THE CELEBRATED JUMPING FROG OF CALAVERAS COUNTY

AND OTHER HUMOROUS TALES

MARK TWAIN

Contents

The Celebrated Jumping Frog of Calaveras County

In compliance with the request of a friend of mine, who wrote me from the East, I called on good-natured, garrulous old Simon Wheeler, and inquired after my friend's friend, *Leonidas W.* Smiley, as requested to do, and I hereunto append the result. I have a lurking suspicion that *Leonidas W.* Smiley is a myth; that my friend never knew such a personage; and that he only conjectured that, if I asked old Wheeler about him, it would remind him of his infamous *Jim* Smiley, and he would go to work and bore me nearly to death with some infernal reminiscence of him as long and tedious as it should be useless to me. If that was the design, it certainly succeeded.

I found Simon Wheeler dozing comfortably by the bar-room stove of the old, dilapidated tavern in the ancient mining camp of Angel's, and I noticed that he was fat and bald-headed, and had an expression of winning gentleness and simplicity upon his tranquil countenance. He roused up and gave me good-day. I told him a friend of mine had commissioned me to make some inquiries about a cherished companion of his boyhood named *Leonidas W.* Smiley—*Rev. Leonidas W.* Smiley—a young minister of the Gospel, who he had heard was at one time a resident of Angel's Camp. I added that, if Mr. Wheeler could tell me anything about this Rev. Leonidas W. Smiley, I would feel under many obligations to him.

Simon Wheeler backed me into a corner and blockaded me

there with his chair, and then sat me down and reeled off the monotonous narrative which follows this paragraph. He never smiled, he never frowned, he never changed his voice from the gentle-flowing key to which he tuned the initial sentence, he never betrayed the slightest suspicion of enthusiasm; but all through the interminable narrative there ran a vein of impressive earnestness and sincerity, which showed me plainly that, so far from his imagining that there was anything ridiculous or funny about his story, he regarded it as a really important matter, and admired its two heroes as men of transcendant genius in *finesse.* To me, the spectacle of a man drifting serenely along through such a queer yarn without ever smiling, was exquisitely absurd. As I said before, I asked him to tell me what he knew of Rev. Leonidas W. Smiley, and he replied as follows. I let him go on in his own way, and never interrupted him once:

THERE WAS A feller here once by the name of *Jim* Smiley, in the winter of '49—or may be it was the spring of '50—I don't recollect exactly, somehow, though what makes me think it was one or the other is because I remember the big flume wasn't finished when he first came to the camp; but any way, he was the curiousest man about always betting on anything that turned up you ever see, if he could get anybody to bet on the other side; and if he couldn't, he'd change sides. Anyway that suited the other man would suit him—anyway just so's he got a bet, *he* was satisfied. But still he was lucky, uncommon lucky; he most always come out winner. He was always ready and laying for a chance; there couldn't be no solit'ry thing mentioned but that feller'd offer to bet on it, and take any side you please, as I was just telling you. If there was a horse-race, you'd find him flush, or you'd find him busted at the end of it; if there was a dog-fight, he'd bet on it; if there was a cat-fight, he'd bet on it; if there was a chicken-fight, he'd bet on it; why, if there was two birds setting on a fence, he would bet you which one would fly first; or if there was a camp-meeting, he would be there reg'lar, to bet on Parson Walker, which he judged to be the best exhorter about here, and so he was, too, and a good man. If he even seen a straddle-bug start to go anywheres, he would bet you how long it would take him to get wherever he was going to, and if you took him up, he would foller that straddle-bug to Mexico but what he would find out where he was bound for and how long he was on the road. Lots of the boys here has seen that Smiley, and can tell you about him. Why, it never made no difference to *him*—he would bet on *any* thing—the dangdest feller. Parson Walker's wife laid very sick once, for a good while, and it seemed as if they warn't going to save her; but one morning he come in, and Smiley asked how she was, and he said she was considerable better—thank the Lord for his inf'nit mercy—and coming on so smart that, with the blessing of Prov'dence, she'd get well yet; and Smiley, before he thought, says, "Well, I'll risk two-and-a-half that she don't, anyway."

Thish-yer Smiley had a mare—the boys called her the fifteen-minute nag, but that was only in fun, you know, because, of course, she was faster than that—and he used to win money on that horse, for all she was so slow and always had the asthma, or the distemper, or the consumption, or something of that kind. They used to give her two or three hundred yards' start, and then pass her under way; but always at the fag-end of the race she'd get excited and desperate-like, and come cavorting and straddling up, and scattering her legs around limber, sometimes in the air, and sometimes out to one side amongst the fences, and kicking up m-o-r-e dust and raising m-o-r-e racket with her coughing and sneezing and blowing her nose—and always fetch up at the stand just about a neck ahead, as near as you could cypher it down.

And he had a little small bull pup, that to look at him you'd think he wan't worth a cent, but to set around and look ornery, and lay for a chance to steal something. But as soon as money was upon him, he was a different dog; his under-jaw'd begin to stick out like the fo'castle of a steamboat, and his teeth would uncover, and shine savage like the furnaces. And a dog might tackle him, and bully-rag him, and bite him, and throw him over his shoulder two or three times, and Andrew Jackson—which was the name of the pup—Andrew Jackson would never let on but what *he* was satisfied, and hadn't expected nothing else—and the bets being doubled and doubled on the other side all the time, till the money was all up; and then all of a sudden he would grab that other dog jest by the j'int of his hind leg and freeze to it—not chaw, you understand, but only jest grip and hang on till they throwed up the sponge, if it was a year. Smiley always come out winner on that pup, till he harnessed a dog once that didn't have no hind legs, because they'd been sawed off by a circular saw, and when the thing had gone along far enough, and the money was all up, and he come to make a snatch for his pet holt, he saw in a minute how he'd been imposed on, and how the other dog had him in the door, so to speak, and he 'peared surprised, and then he looked sorter discouraged-like, and didn't try no more to win the fight, and so he got shucked out bad. He give Smiley a look, as much as to say his heart was broke, and it was *his* fault, for putting up a dog that hadn't no hind legs for him to take holt of, which was his main dependance in a fight, and then he limped off a piece and laid down and died. It was a good pup, was that Andrew Jackson, and would have made a name for hisself if he'd lived, for the stuff was in him, and he had genius—I know it, because he hadn't had no opportunities to speak of, and it don't stand to reason that a dog could make such a fight as he could under them circumstances, if he hadn't no talent. It always makes me feel sorry when I think of that last fight of his'n, and the way it turned out.

Well, thish-yer Smiley had rat-tarriers, and chicken cocks, and tom-cats, and all them kind of things, till you couldn't rest, and you couldn't fetch nothing for him to bet on but he'd match you. He ketched a frog one day, and took him home, and said he cal'klated to educate him; and so he never done nothing for three months but set in his back yard and learn that frog to jump. And you bet you he *did* learn him, too. He'd give him a little punch behind, and the next minute you'd see that frog whirling in the air like it doughnut—see him turn one summerset, or may be a couple, if he got a good start, and come down flat-footed and all right, like a cat. He got him up so in the matter of catching flies, and kept him in practice so constant, that he'd nail a fly every time as far as he could see him. Smiley said all a frog wanted was education, and he could do most anything—and I believe him. Why, I've seen him set Dan'l Webster down here on this floor—Dan'l Webster was the name of the frog—and sing out, "Flies, Dan'l, flies!" and quicker'n you could wink, he'd spring straight up, and snake a fly off'n the counter there, and flop down on the floor again as solid as a gob of mud, and fall to scratching the side of his head with his hind foot as indifferent as if he hadn't no idea he'd been doin' any more'n any frog might do. You never see a frog so modest and straightfor'ard as he was, for all he was so gifted. And when it come to fair and square jumping on a dead level, he could get over more ground at one straddle than any animal of his breed you ever see. Jumping on a dead level was his strong suit, you understand; and when it come to that, Smiley would ante up money on him as long as he had a red. Smiley was monstrous proud of his frog, and well he might be, for fellers that had traveled and been everywheres, all said he laid over any frog that ever *they* see.

Well, Smiley kept the beast in a little lattice box, and he used to fetch him down town sometimes and lay for a bet. One day a feller—a stranger in the camp, he was—come across him with his box, and says:

"What might it be that you've got in the box?"

And Smiley says, sorter indifferent like, "It might be a parrot, or it might be a canary, maybe, but it an't—it's only just a frog."

And the feller took it, and looked at it careful, and turned it round this way and that, and says, "H'm—so 'tis. Well, what's *he* good for?"

"Well," Smiley says, easy and careless, "he's good enough for *one* thing, I should judge—he can outjump ary frog in Calaveras county."

The feller took the box again, and took another long, particular look, and give it back to Smiley, and says, very deliberate, "Well, I don't see no p'ints about that frog that's any better'n any other frog."

"Maybe you don't," Smiley says. "Maybe you understand frogs, and maybe you don't understand 'em; maybe you've had experience, and maybe you an't only a amature, as it were. Anyways, I've got *my* opinion, and I'll risk forty dollars that he can outjump any frog in Calaveras county."

And the feller studied a minute, and then says, kinder sad like, "Well, I'm only a stranger here, and I an't got no frog; but if I had a frog, I'd bet you."

And then Smiley says, "That's all right—that's all right—if you'll hold my box a minute, I'll go and get you a frog." And so the feller took the box, and put up his forty dollars along with Smiley's and set down to wait.

So he set there a good while thinking and thinking to hisself, and then he got the frog out and prized his mouth open and took a teaspoon and filled him full of quail shot—filled him pretty near up to his chin—and set him on the floor. Smiley he went to the swamp and slopped around in the mud for a long time, and finally he ketched a frog, and fetched him in, and give him to this feller, and says:

"Now, if you're ready, set him alongside of Dan'l, with his fore-paws just even with Dan'l, and I'll give the word." Then he says, "One—two—three—jump!" and him and the feller touched up the frogs from behind, and the new frog hopped off, but Dan'l give a heave, and hysted up his shoulders—so—like a Frenchman, but it wan't no use—he couldn't budge; he was planted as solid as an anvil, and he couldn't no more stir than if he was anchored out. Smiley was a good deal surprised, and he was disgusted too, but he didn't have no idea what the matter was, of course.

The feller took the money and started away; and when he was going out at the door, he sorter jerked his thumb over his shoulder—this way—at Dan'l, and says again, very deliberate, "Well *I* don't see no p'ints about that frog that's any better'n any other frog."

Smiley he stood scratching his head and looking down at Dan'l a long time, and at last he says, "I do wonder what in the nation that frog throw'd off for—I wonder if there an't something the matter with him—he 'pears to look mighty baggy, somehow." And he ketched Dan'l by the nap of the neck, and lifted him up and says, "Why, blame my cats, if he don't weigh five pound!" and turned him upside down, and he belched out a double handful of shot. And then he see how it was, and he was the maddest man—he set the frog down and took out after that feller, but he never ketched him. And——

[Here Simon Wheeler heard his name called from the front

yard, and got up to see what was wanted.] And turning to me as he moved away, he said: “just set where you are, stranger, and rest easy—I an't going to be gone a second.”

But, by your leave, I did not think that a continuation of the history of the enterprising vagabond *Jim* Smiley would be likely to afford me much information concerning the Rev. *Leonidas W.* Smiley, and so I started away.

At the door I met the sociable Wheeler returning, and he button-holed me and recommenced:

“Well, thish-yer Smiley had a yaller one-eyed cow that didn't have no tail, only jest a short stump like a bannanner, and——”

“Oh! hang Smiley and his afflicted cow!” I muttered, good-naturedly, and bidding the old gentleman good day, I departed.

1865

FROM

PRIVATE HISTORY OF THE "JUMPING FROG" STORY BY MARK TWAIN*

A FEW WEEKS ago Professor Van Dyke, of Princeton, asked this question:

"Do you know how old your Jumping Frog story is?"

And I answered:

"Yes—forty-five years. The thing happened in Calaveras County in the spring of 1849."

"No; it happened earlier—a couple of thousand years earlier; it is a Greek story."

I was astonished—and hurt. I said:

"I am willing to be a literary thief if it has been so ordained; I am even willing to be caught robbing the ancient dead alongside of Hopkinson Smith,** for he is my friend and a good fellow, and I think would be as honest as any one if he could do it without occasioning remark; but I am not willing to antedate his crimes by fifteen hundred years. I must ask you to knock off part of that."

But the professor was not chaffing; he was in earnest and could not abate a century. He named the Greek author, and offered to get the book and send it to me and the college text

---

* First published in *The North American Review*, Apr., 1894, Vol. 158, No. 449, pp. 446–453.

** A fellow writer.

book containing the English translation also. I thought I would like the translation best, because Greek makes me tired. January 30th he sent me the English version, and I will presently insert it in this article. It is my Jumping Frog tale in every essential. It is not strung out as I have strung it out, but it is all there.

To me this is very curious and interesting. Curious, for several reasons. For instance:

I heard the story told by a man who was not telling it to his hearers as a thing new to them, but as a thing which *they had witnessed and would remember.* He was a dull person, and ignorant; he had no gift as a story-teller, and no invention; in his mouth this episode was merely history—history and statistics; and the gravest sort of history, too; he was entirely serious, for he was dealing with what to him were austere facts, and they interested him solely because they *were* facts; he was drawing on his memory, not his mind; he saw no humor in his tale, neither did his listeners; neither he nor they ever smiled or laughed; in my time I have not attended a more solemn conference. To him and to his fellow gold-miners there were just two things in the story that were worth considering. One was, the smartness of its hero, Jim Smiley, in taking the stranger in with a loaded frog; and the other was Smiley's deep knowledge of a frog's nature—for he knew (as the narrator asserted and the listeners conceded) that a frog *likes shot* and is always ready to eat it. Those men discussed those two points, and those only. They were hearty in their admiration of them, and none of the party was aware that a first rate story had been told, in a first rate way, and that it was brimful of a quality whose presence they never suspected—humor.

Now, then, the interesting question is, *did* the frog episode happen in Angel's Camp in the spring of '49, as told in my hearing that day in the fall of 1865? I am perfectly sure that it did. I am also sure that its duplicate happened in Bœotia a couple of thousand years ago. I think it must be a case of history actually repeating itself, and not a case of a good story floating down the ages and surviving because too good to be allowed to perish.

I would now like to have the reader examine the Greek story and the story told by the dull and solemn Californian, and observe how exactly alike they are in essentials.

[*Translation.*]

THE ATHENIAN AND THE FROG.*

An Athenian once fell in with a Bœotian who was sitting by the road side looking at a frog. Seeing the other approach, the Bœotian said his was a remarkable frog, and asked if he would agree to start a contest of frogs, on condition that he whose frog jumped farthest should receive a large sum of money. The Athenian replied that he would if the other would fetch him a frog, for the lake was near. To this he agreed, and when he was gone the Athenian took the frog, and opening its mouth poured some stones into its stomach, so that it did not indeed seem larger than before, but could not jump. The Bœotian soon returned with the other frog, and the contest began. The second frog first was pinched and jumped moderately; then they pinched the Bœotian frog. And he gathered himself for a leap, and used the utmost effort, but he could not move his body the least. So the Athenian departed with the money. When he was gone the Bœotian, wondering what was the matter with the frog, lifted him up and examined him. And being turned upside down, he opened his mouth and vomited out the stones.

And here is the way it happened in California:

---

* Sidgwick, *Greek Prose Composition*, page 116.

FROM "THE CELEBRATED JUMPING FROG OF CALAVERAS COUNTY."

Well, thish-yer Smiley had rat-tarriers, and chicken cocks, and tom cats, and all them kind of things, till you couldn't rest, and you couldn't fetch nothing for him to bet on but he'd match you. He ketched a frog one day, and took him home, and said he cal'lated to educate him; and so he never done nothing for three months but set in his backyard and learn that frog to jump. And you bet you he *did* learn him, too. He'd give him a little punch behind, and the next minute you'd see that frog whirling in the air like a doughnut—see him turn one summerset, or maybe a couple if he got a good start, and come down flat-footed and all right, like a cat. He got him up so in the matter of ketching flies, and kep' him in practice so constant, that he'd nail a fly every time as fur as he could see him. Smiley said all a frog wanted was education, and he could do 'most anything—and I believe him. Why, I've seen him set Dan'l Webster down here on this floor—Dan'l Webster was the name of the frog—and sing out "Flies, Dan'l, flies!" and quicker'n you could wink he'd spring straight up and snake a fly off'n the counter there, and flop down on the floor ag'in as solid as a gob of mud, and fall to scratching the side of his head with his hind foot as indifferent as if he hadn't no idea he'd been doin' any more'n any frog might do. You never see a frog so modest and straightfor'ard as he was, for all he was so gifted. And when it come to fair and square jumping on a dead level, he could get over more ground at one straddle than any animal of his breed you ever see. Jumping on a dead level was his strong suit, you understand; and when it come to that, Smiley would ante up money on him as long as he had a red. Smiley was monstrous proud of his frog, and well he might be, for fellers that had travelled and been everywheres, all said he laid over any frog that ever *they* see.

Well, Smiley kep' the beast in a little lattice box, and he used to fetch him downtown sometimes and lay for a bet. One day a feller—a stranger in the camp, he was—come acrost him with his box, and says:

"What might it be that you've got in the box?"

And Smiley says, sorter indifferent-like, "It might be a parrot, or it might be a canary, maybe, but it ain't—it's only just a frog."

And the feller took it, and looked at it careful, and turned it round this way and that, and says, "H'm—so 'tis. Well, what's *he* good for?"

"Well," Smiley says, easy and careless, "he's good enough for *one* thing, I should judge—he can outjump any frog in Calaveras County."

The feller took the box again and took another long, particular look, and give it back to Smiley and says very deliberate, "Well," he says, " I don't see no p'ints about that frog that's any better'n any other frog."

"Maybe you don't," Smiley says. "Maybe you understand frogs and maybe you don't understand 'em; maybe you've had experience, and maybe you ain't only a amature, as it were. Anyways, I've got *my* opinion and I'll resk forty dollars that he can outjump any frog in Calaveras County."

And the feller studies a minute and then says, kinder sad like, "Well, I'm only a stranger here, and I ain't got no frog, but if I had a frog I'd bet you."

And then Smiley says: "That's all right—that's all right—if you'll hold my box a minute, I'll go and get you a frog." And so the feller took the box and put up his forty dollars along with Smiley's and set down to wait. So he set there a good while thinking and thinking to hisself, and then he got the frog out and prized his mouth open and took a teaspoon and filled him full of quail shot—filled him pretty near up to his chin—and set him on the floor. Smiley he went to the swamp and slopped around in the mud for a long time, and finally he ketched a frog and fetched him in and give him to this feller, and says:

"Now, if you're ready, set him alongside of Dan'l, with his fore-paws just even with Danl's, and I'll give the word." Then he says, "One—two—three—*git!*" and him and the feller touched up the frogs from behind, and the new frog hopped off lively; but Dan'l give a heave, and hysted up his shoulders—so—like a Frenchman, but it warn't no use—he couldn't budge; he was planted as solid as a church, and he couldn't no more stir than if he was anchored out. Smiley was a good deal surprised, and he was disgusted, too, but he didn't have no idea what the matter was, of course.

The feller took the money and started away; and when he was going out at the door, he sorter jerked his thumb over his shoulder—so—at Dan'l, and says again, very deliberate: "Well," he says, "*I* don't see no p'ints about that frog that's any better'n any other frog."

Smiley he stood scratching his head and looking down at Dan'l a long time, and at last he says, "I do wonder what in the nation that frog throw'd off for—I wonder if there ain't something the matter with him—he 'pears to look mighty baggy, somehow." And he ketched Dan'l by the nap of the neck, and hefted him, and says, "Why, blame my cats if he don't weigh five pound!" and turned him upside down and he belched out a double handful of shot. And then he see how it was, and he was the maddest man—he set the frog down and took out after that feller, but he never ketched him.

The resemblances are deliciously exact. There you have the

wily Bœotian and the wily Jim Smiley waiting—two thousand years apart—and waiting, each equipped with his frog and "laying" for the stranger. A contest is proposed—for money. The Athenian would take a chance "if the other would fetch him a frog"; the Yankee says: "I'm only a stranger here and I ain't got no frog; but if I had a frog I'd bet you." The wily Bœotian and the wily Californian, with that vast gulf of two thousand years between, retire eagerly and go frogging in the marsh; the Athenian and the Yankee remain behind and work a base advantage, the one with pebbles, the other with shot. Presently the contest began. In the one case "they pinched the Bœotian frog"; in the other, "him and the feller touched up the frogs from behind." The Bœotian frog "gathered himself for a leap" (you can just *see* him!), but "could not move his body in the least"; the Californian frog "give a heave, but it warn't no use—he couldn't budge." In both the ancient and the modern cases the strangers departed with the money. The Bœotian and the Californian wonder what is the matter with their frogs; they lift them and examine; they turn them upside down and out spills the informing ballast.

Yes, the resemblances are curiously exact. I used to tell the story of the Jumping Frog in San Francisco, and presently Artemus Ward came along and wanted it to help fill out a little book which he was about to publish; so I wrote it out and sent it to his publisher, Carleton; but Carleton thought the book had enough matter in it, so he gave the story to Henry Clapp as a present, and Clapp put it in his *Saturday Press*, and it killed that paper with a suddenness that was beyond praise. At least the paper died with that issue, and none but envious people have ever tried to rob me of the honor and credit of killing it. The "Jumping Frog" was the first piece of writing of mine that spread itself through the newspapers and brought me into public notice.

Consequently, the *Saturday Press* was a cocoon and I the worm in it; also, I was the gay-colored literary moth which its death set free. This simile has been used before.

Early in '66 the "Jumping Frog" was issued in book form, with other sketches of mine. A year or two later Madame Blanc translated it into French and published it in the *Revue des Deux Mondes,* but the result was not what should have been expected, for the *Revue* struggled along and pulled through, and is alive yet. I think the fault must have been in the translation. I ought to have translated it myself. I think so because I examined into the matter and finally retranslated the sketch from the French back into English, to see what the trouble was; that is, to see just what sort of a focus the French people got upon it. Then the mystery was explained. In French the story is too confused, and chaotic, and unreposeful, and ungrammatical, and insane; consequently it could only cause grief and sickness—it could not kill. A glance at my retranslation will show the reader that this must be true.

[*My Retranslation.*]

THE FROG JUMPING OF THE COUNTY OF CALAVERAS.

Eh bien! this Smiley nourished some terriers á rats, and some cocks of combat, and some cats, and all sort of things; and with his rage of betting one no had more of repose. He trapped one day a frog and him imported with him *(et l'emporta chez lui)* saying that he pretended to make his edcation. You me believe if you will, but during three months he not has nothing done but to him apprehend to jump *(apprendre a sauter)* in a court retired of her mansion *(de sa maison).* And I you respond that he have succeeded. He him gives a small blow by behind, and the instant after you shall see the frog turn in the air like a grease-biscuit, make one summer sault, sometimes two, when she was well started, and re-fall upon his feet like a cat. He him had accomplished in the art of to gobble the flies *(gober des mouches),* and him there exercised continually—so well that a fly at the most far that she appeared was a fly lost. Smiley had custom to say that all which lacked to a frog it was the education, but with the education she could do nearly all—and I him believe. *Tenez,* I him have seen pose Daniel Webster there upon this plank—Daniel Webster was the name of the frog—and to him sing, "Some flies, Daniel, some flies!"—in a flash of the eye Daniel had bounded and seized a fly here upon the counter, then jumped anew at the earth, where he rested truly to himself scratch the head with his behind-foot, as if he no had not the least idea of his superiority. Never you not have seen frog as modest, as natural, sweet as she was. And when he himself agitated to jump purely and simply upon plain earth, she does more ground in one jump than any beast of his species than you can know.

To jump plain—this was his strong. When he himself agitated for that Smiley multiplied the bets upon her as long as there to him remained a red. It must to know, Smiley was monstrously proud of his frog, and he of it was right, for some men who were traveled, who had all seen, said that they to him would be injurious to him compare to another frog. Smiley guarded Daniel in a little box latticed which he carried bytimes to the village for some bet.

One day an individual stranger at the camp him arrested with his box and him said:

"What is this that you have then shut up there within?"

Smiley said, with an air indifferent:

"That could be a paroquet, or a syringe *(ou un serin),* but this no is nothing of such, it not is but a frog."

The individual it took, it regarded with care, it turned from one side and from the other, then he said:

"*Tiens!* in effect!—At what is she good?"

"My God!" respond Smiley, always with an air disengaged, "she is good for one thing, to my notice, *(à mon avis),* she can batter in jumping *(elle peut batter en sautant)* all frogs of the county of Calaveras."

The individual re-took the box, it examined of new longly, and it rendered to Smiley in saying with an air deliberate:

"*Eh bien!* I no saw not that that frog had nothing of better than each frog." *(Je ne vois pas que cette grenouille ait rien de mieux qu'aucune grenouille).* [If that isn't grammar gone to seed, then I count myself no judge.—M. T.]

"Possible that you not it saw not," said Smiley, "possible that you—you comprehend frogs; possible that you not you there comprehend nothing; possible that you had of the experience, and possible that you not be but an amateur. Of all manner *(De toute manière)* I bet forty dollars that she batter in jumping no matter which frog of the county of Calaveras."

The individual reflected a second, and said like sad: "I not am but a stranger here, I no have not a frog; but if I of it had one, I would embrace the bet."

"Strong, well!" respond Smiley; "nothing of more facility. If you will hold my box a minute, I go you to search a frog *(j'irai vous chercher).*"

Behold, then, the individual, who guards the box, who puts his forty dollars upon those of Smiley, and who attends *(et qui attend).* He attended enough longtimes, reflecting all solely. And figure you that he takes Daniel, him opens the mouth by force and with a tea-spoon him fills with shot of the hunt, even him fills just to the chin, then he him puts by the earth. Smiley during these times was at slopping in a swamp. Finally he trapped *(attrape)* a frog, him carried to that individual, and said:

"Now if you be ready, put him all against Daniel, with their before-feet upon the same line, and I give the signal"—then he added: "One, two, three—advance!"

Him and the individual touched their frogs by behind, and the frog new put to jump smartly, but Daniel himself lifted ponderously, exalted the shoulders thus, like a Frenchman—to what good? he could not budge, he is planted solid like a church, he not advance no more than if one him had put at the anchor.

Smiley was surprised and disgusted, but he not himself doubted not of the turn being intended *(mais il ne se doutait pas du tour bien entendu).* The individual empocketed the silver, himself with it went, and of it himself in going is that he no gives not a jerk of thumb over the shoulder—like that—at the poor Daniel, in saying with his air deliberate—*(L'individu empoche l'argent s'en va et en s'en allant est ce qu'il ne donne pas un coup de pouce par-dessus l'épaule, comme ça, au pauvre Daniel, en disant de son air délibéré.)*

"*Eh bien!* I no see not that that frog has nothing of better than an other."

Smiley himself scratched longtimes the head, the eyes fixed upon Daniel, until that which at last he said:

"I me demand how the devil it makes itself that this beast has refused. Is it that she had something? One would believe that she is stuffed."

He grasped Daniel by the skin of the neck, him lifted and said:

"The wolf me bite if he no weigh not five pounds."

He him reversed and the unhappy belched two handfuls of shot (*et le malheureux,* etc).—When Smiley recognized how it was, he was like mad. He deposited his frog by the earth and ran after that individual, but he not him caught never.

It may be that there are people who can translate better than I can, but I am not acquainted with them.

So ends the private and public history of the jumping frog of Calaveras County, an incident which has this unique feature about it—that it is both old and new, a "chestnut" and not a "chestnut"; for it was original when it happened two thousand years ago, and was again original when it happened in California in our own time.

1894

CODA 1903

When I became convinced that the "Jumping Frog" was a Greek story two or three thousand years old, I was sincerely happy, for apparently here was a most striking and satisfactory justification of a favorite theory of mine—to wit, that no occurrence is sole and solitary, but is merely a repetition of a thing which has happened before, and perhaps often...By-and-by, in England, after a few years, I learned that there hadn't been any Greek frog in the business, and no Greek story about his adventures. Professor Sidgwick had not claimed that it was a Greek tale; he had merely synopsized the Calaveras tale and transferred the incident to classic Greece; but as he did not state that it was the same old frog, the English papers reproved him for the omission. He told me this in England in 1899 or 1900, and was much troubled about that censure, for his act had been innocent, he believing that the story's origin was so well known as to render formal mention of it unnecessary.*

* Twain, Mark & Strothman, F. (Illustrator) (1903). *The Jumping Frog: In English, Then in French, and Then Clawed Back into a Civilized Language Once More by Patient, Unremunerated Toil* (MCMIII ed.). New York and London: Harper & Brothers, Publishers. pp. 64–66.

Cannibalism in the Cars

I visited St. Louis lately, and on my way West, after changing cars at Terre Haute, Indiana, a mild, benevolent-looking gentleman of about forty-five, or maybe fifty, came in at one of the way-stations and sat down beside me. We talked together pleasantly on various subjects for an hour, perhaps, and I found him exceedingly intelligent and entertaining. When he learned that I was from Washington, he immediately began to ask questions about various public men, and about Congressional affairs; and I saw very shortly that I was conversing with a man who was perfectly familiar with the ins and outs of political life at the Capital, even to the ways and manners, and customs of procedure of Senators and Representatives in the Chambers of the national Legislature. Presently two men halted near us for a single moment, and one said to the other:

"Harris, if you'll do that for me, I'll never forget you, my boy."

My new comrade's eye lighted pleasantly. The words had touched upon a happy memory, I thought. Then his face settled into thoughtfulness—almost into gloom. He turned to me and said, "Let me tell you a story; let me give you a secret chapter of my life—a chapter that has never been referred to by me since its events transpired. Listen patiently, and promise that you will not interrupt me."

I said I would not, and he related the following strange adventure, speaking sometimes with animation, sometimes with melancholy, but always with feeling and earnestness.

On the 19th of December, 1853, I started from St. Louis on the evening train bound for Chicago. There were only twenty-four passengers, all told. There were no ladies and no children. We were in excellent spirits, and pleasant acquaintanceships were soon formed. The journey bade fair to be a happy one; and no individual in the party, I think, had even the vaguest presentiment of the horrors we were soon to undergo.

At 11 P.M. it began to snow hard. Shortly after leaving the small village of Welden, we entered upon that tremendous prairie solitude that stretches its leagues on leagues of houseless dreariness far away toward the Jubilee Settlements. The winds, unobstructed by trees or hills, or even vagrant rocks, whistled fiercely, across the level desert, driving the falling snow before it like spray from the crested waves of a stormy sea. The snow was deepening fast; and we knew, by the diminished speed of the train, that the engine was plowing through it with steadily increasing difficulty. Indeed, it almost came to a dead halt sometimes, in the midst of great drifts that piled themselves like colossal graves across the track. Conversation began to flag. Cheerfulness gave place to grave concern. The possibility of being imprisoned in the snow, on the bleak prairie, fifty miles from any house, presented itself to every mind, and extended its depressing influence over every spirit.

At two o'clock in the morning I was aroused out of an uneasy slumber by the ceasing of all motion about me. The appalling truth flashed upon me instantly—we were captives in a snowdrift! "All hands to the rescue!" Every man sprang to obey. Out into the wild night, the pitchy darkness, the billowy snow, the driving storm, every soul leaped, with the consciousness that a moment lost now might bring destruction to us all. Shovels, hands, boards—anything, everything that could displace snow, was brought into instant requisition. It was a weird picture, that small company of frantic men fighting the banking snows, half in the blackest shadow and half in the angry light of the locomotive's reflector.

One short hour sufficed to prove the utter uselessness of our efforts. The storm barricaded the track with a dozen drifts while we dug one away. And worse than this, it was discovered that the last grand charge the engine had made upon the enemy had broken the fore-and-aft shaft of the driving-wheel! With a free track before us we should still have been helpless. We entered the car wearied with labor, and very sorrowful. We gathered about the stoves, and gravely canvassed our situation. We had no provisions whatever—in this lay our chief distress. We could not freeze, for there was a good supply of wood in the tender. This was our only comfort. The discussion ended at last in accepting the disheartening decision of the conductor, *viz.*, that it would be death for any man to attempt to travel fifty miles on foot through snow like that. We could not send for help, and even if we could it would not come. We must submit, and await, as patiently as we might, succor or starvation! I think the stoutest heart there felt a momentary chill when those words were uttered.

Within the hour conversation subsided to a low murmur here and there about the car, caught fitfully between the rising and falling of the blast; the lamps grew dim; and the majority of the castaways settled themselves among the flickering shadows to think—to forget the present, if they could—to sleep, if they might.

The eternal night—it surely seemed eternal to us—wore its lagging hours away at last, and the cold gray dawn broke in the east. As the light grew stronger the passengers began to stir and give signs of life, one after another, and each in turn pushed his slouched hat up from his forehead, stretched his stiffened limbs, and glanced out of the windows upon the cheerless prospect.

It was cheerless, indeed!—not a living thing visible anywhere, not a human habitation; nothing but a vast white desert; uplifted sheets of snow drifted hither and thither before the wind—a world of eddying flakes shutting out the firmament above.

All day we moped about the cars, saying little, thinking much. Another lingering dreary night—and hunger.

Another dawning—another day of silence, sadness, wasting hunger, hopeless watching for succor that could not come. A night of restless slumber, filled with dreams of feasting—wakings distressed with the gnawings of hunger.

The fourth day came and went—and the fifth! Five days of dreadful imprisonment! A savage hunger looked out at every eye. There was in it a sign of awful import—the foreshadowing of a something that was vaguely shaping itself in every heart—a something which no tongue dared yet to frame into words.

The sixth day passed—the seventh dawned upon as gaunt and haggard and hopeless a company of men as ever stood in the shadow of death. It must out now! That thing which had been growing up in every heart was ready to leap from every lip at last! Nature had been taxed to the utmost—she must yield. RICHARD H. GASTON of Minnesota, tall, cadaverous, and pale, rose up. All knew what was coming. All prepared—every emotion, every semblance of excitement was smothered—only a calm, thoughtful seriousness appeared in the eyes that were lately so wild.

"Gentlemen: It cannot be delayed longer! The time is at hand! We must determine which of us shall die to furnish food for the rest!"

MR. JOHN J. WILLIAMS of Illinois rose and said: "Gentlemen—I nominate the Rev. James Sawyer of Tennessee."

MR. WM. R. ADAMS of Indiana said: "I nominate Mr. Daniel

Slote of New York."

MR. CHARLES J. LANGDON: "I nominate Mr. Samuel A. Bowen of St. Louis."

MR. SLOTE: "Gentlemen—I desire to decline in favor of Mr. John A. Van Nostrand, Jun., of New Jersey."

MR. GASTON: "If there be no objection, the gentleman's desire will be acceded to."

MR. VAN NOSTRAND objecting, the resignation of Mr. Slote was rejected. The resignations of Messrs. Sawyer and Bowen were also offered, and refused upon the same grounds.

MR. A. L. BASCOM of Ohio: "I move that the nominations now close, and that the House proceed to an election by ballot."

MR. SAWYER: "Gentlemen—I protest earnestly against these proceedings. They are, in every way, irregular and unbecoming. I must beg to move that they be dropped at once, and that we elect a chairman of the meeting and proper officers to assist him, and then we can go on with the business before us understandingly."

MR. BELL of Iowa: "Gentlemen—I object. This is no time to stand upon forms and ceremonious observances. For more than seven days we have been without food. Every moment we lose in idle discussion increases our distress. I am satisfied with the nominations that have been made—every gentleman present is, I believe—and I, for one, do not see why we should not proceed at once to elect one or more of them. I wish to offer a resolution—"

MR. GASTON: "It would be objected to, and have to lie over one day under the rules, thus bringing about the very delay you wish to avoid. The gentleman from New Jersey—"

MR. VAN NOSTRAND: "Gentlemen—I am a stranger among you; I have not sought the distinction that has been conferred upon me, and I feel a delicacy—"

MR. MORGAN of Alabama (interrupting): "I move the previous question."

The motion was carried, and further debate shut off, of course. The motion to elect officers was passed, and under it Mr. Gaston was chosen chairman, Mr. Blake, secretary, Messrs. Holcomb, Dyer, and Baldwin a committee on nominations, and Mr. R. M. Howland, purveyor, to assist the committee in making selections.

A recess of half an hour was then taken, and some little caucusing followed. At the sound of the gavel the meeting assembled, and the committee reported in favor of Messrs. George Ferguson of Kentucky, Lucien Herrman of Louisiana, and W. Messick of Colorado as candidates. The report was accepted.

MR. ROGERS of Missouri: "Mr. President—The report being properly before the House now, I move to amend it by substituting for the name of Mr. Herrman that of Mr. Lucius Harris of St. Louis, who is well and honorably known to us all. I do not wish to be understood as casting the least reflection upon the high character and standing of the gentleman from Louisiana—far from it. I respect and esteem him as much as any gentleman here present possibly can; but none of us can be blind to the fact that he had lost more flesh during the week that we have lain here than any among us—none of us can be blind to the fact that the committee has been derelict in its duty, either through negligence or a graver fault, in thus offering for our suffrages a gentleman who, however pure his own motives may be, has really less nutriment in him—"

THE CHAIR: "The gentleman from Missouri will take his seat. The Chair cannot allow the integrity of the committee to be questioned save by the regular course, under the rules. What action will the House take upon the gentleman's motion?"

MR. HALLIDAY of Virginia: "I move to further amend the report by substituting Mr. Harvey Davis of Oregon for Mr. Messick. It may be urged by gentlemen that the hardships and privations of a frontier life have rendered Mr. Davis tough; but, gentlemen, is this a time to cavil at toughness? Is this a time to be fastidious concerning trifles? Is this a time to dispute about matters of paltry significance? No, gentlemen, bulk is what we desire, substance, weight, bulk—these are the supreme requisites now—not talent, not genius, not education. I insist upon my motion."

MR. MORGAN *(excitedly):* "Mr. Chairman—I do most strenuously object to this amendment. The gentleman from Oregon is old, and furthermore is bulky only in bone—not in flesh. I ask the gentleman from Virginia if it is soup we want instead of solid sustenance? if he would delude us with shadows? if he would mock our suffering with an Oregonian specter? I ask him if he can look upon the anxious faces around him, if he can gaze into our sad eyes, if he can listen to the beating of our expectant hearts, and still thrust this famine-stricken fraud upon us? I ask him if he can think of our desolate state, of our past sorrows, of our dark future, and still unpityingly foist upon us this wreck, this ruin, this tottering swindle, this gnarled and blighted and sapless vagabond from Oregon's inhospitable shores? Never!" [*Applause.*]

The amendment was put to vote, after a fiery debate, and lost. Mr. Harris was substituted on the first amendment. The balloting then began. Five ballots were held without a choice. On the sixth, Mr. Harris was elected, all voting for him but himself. It was then moved that his election should be ratified by acclamation, which was lost, in consequence of his again voting against himself.

MR. RADWAY moved that the House now take up the remaining candidates, and go into an election for breakfast. This was carried.

On the first ballot there was a tie, half the members favoring one candidate on account of his youth, and half favoring the other on account of his superior size. The President gave the casting vote for the latter, Mr. Messick. This decision created considerable dissatisfaction among the friends of Mr. Ferguson, the defeated candidate, and there was some talk of demanding a new ballot; but in the midst of it a motion to adjourn was carried, and the meeting broke up at once.

The preparations for supper diverted the attention of the Ferguson faction from the discussion of their grievance for a long time, and then, when they would have taken it up again, the happy announcement that Mr. Harris was ready drove all thought of it to the winds.

We improvised tables by propping up the backs of car-seats, and sat down with hearts full of gratitude to the finest supper that had blessed our vision for seven torturing days. How changed we were from what we had been a few short hours before! Hopeless, sad-eyed misery, hunger, feverish anxiety, desperation, then; thankfulness, serenity, joy too deep for utterance now. That I know was the cheeriest hour of my eventful life. The winds howled, and blew the snow wildly about our prison-house, but they were powerless to distress us any more. I liked Harris. He might have been better done, perhaps, but I am free to say that no man ever agreed with me better than Harris, or afforded me so large a degree of satisfaction. Messick was very well, though rather high-flavored, but for genuine nutritiousness and delicacy of fiber, give me Harris. Messick had his good points—I will not attempt to deny it, nor do I wish to do it—but he was no more fitted for breakfast than a mummy would be, sir—not a bit.

Lean?—why, bless me!—and tough? Ah, he was very tough! You could not imagine it—you could never imagine anything like it.

"Do you mean to tell me that—"

"Do not interrupt me, please. After breakfast we elected a man by the name of Walker, from Detroit, for supper. He was very good. I wrote his wife so afterward. He was worthy of all praise. I shall always remember Walker. He was a little rare, but very good. And then the next morning we had Morgan of Alabama for breakfast. He was one of the finest men I ever sat down to—handsome, educated, refined, spoke several languages fluently—a perfect gentleman—he was a perfect gentleman, and singularly juicy. For supper we had that Oregon patiarch, and he *was* a fraud, there is no question about it—old, scraggy, tough, nobody can picture the reality. I finally said, gentlemen, you can do as you like, but *I* will wait for another election. And Grimes of Illinois said, 'Gentlemen, *I* will wait also. When you elect a man that has *something* to recommend him, I shall be glad to join you again.' It soon became evident that there was general dissatisfaction with Davis of Oregon, and so, to preserve the good will that had prevailed so pleasantly since we had had Harris, an election was called, and the result of it was that Baker of Georgia was chosen. He was splendid! Well, well—after that we had Doolittle, and Hawkins, and McElroy (there was some complaint about McElroy, because he was uncommonly short and thin), and Penrod, and two Smiths, and Bailey (Bailey had a wooden leg, which was clear loss, but he was otherwise good), and an Indian boy, and an organ-grinder, and a gentleman by the name of Buckminster—a poor stick of a vagabond that wasn't any good for company and no account for breakfast. We were glad we got him elected before relief came."

"And so the blessed relief *did* come at last?"

"Yes, it came one bright, sunny morning, just after election.

John Murphy was the choice, and there never was a better, I am willing to testify; but John Murphy came home with us, in the train that came to succor us, and lived to marry the widow Harris—"

"Relict of—"

"Relict of our first choice. He married her, and is happy and respected and prosperous yet. Ah, it was like a novel, sir—it was like a romance. This is my stopping-place, sir; I must bid you good-by. Any time that you can make it convenient to tarry a day or two with me, I shall be glad to have you. I like you, sir; I have conceived an affection for you. I could like you as well as I liked Harris himself, sir. Good day, sir, and a pleasant journey."

He was gone. I never felt so stunned, so distressed, so bewildered in my life. But in my soul I was glad he was gone. With all his gentleness of manner and his soft voice, I shuddered whenever he turned his hungry eye upon me; and when I heard that I had achieved his perilous affection, and that I stood almost with the late Harris in his esteem, my heart fairly stood still!

I was bewildered beyond description. I did not doubt his word; I could not question a single item in a statement so stamped with the earnestness of truth as his; but its dreadful details overpowered me, and threw my thoughts into hopeless confusion. I saw the conductor looking at me. I said, "Who is that man?"

"He was a member of Congress once, and a good one. But he got caught in a snow-drift in the cars, and like to have been starved to death. He got so frost-bitten and frozen up generally, and used up for want of something to eat, that he was sick and out of his head two or three months afterward. He is all right now, only he is a monomaniac, and when he gets on that old subject he never stops till he has eat up that whole car-load of people he talks about. He would have finished the crowd by this time, only he had to get out here. He had got their names as pat as A B C. When he gets all eat up but himself, he always says: 'Then the hour for the usual election for breakfast having arrived, and there being no opposition, I was duly elected, after which, there being no objections offered, I resigned. Thus I am here.'"

I felt inexpressibly relieved to know that I had only been listening to the harmless vagaries of a madman instead of the genuine experiences of a bloodthirsty cannibal.

1868

Journalism in Tennessee

The Editor of the Memphis *Avalanche* swoops thus mildly down upon a correspondent who posted him as a Radical:—"While he was writing the first word, the middle, dotting his i's, crossing his t's, and punching his period, he knew he was concocting a sentence that was saturated with infamy and reeking with falsehoods." *Exchange*

I was told by the physician that a Southern climate would improve my health, and so I went down to Tennessee, and got a berth on the *Morning Glory and Johnson County War-Whoop* as associate editor. When I went on duty I found the chief editor sitting tilted back in a three-legged chair with his feet on a pine table. There was another pine table in the room and another afflicted chair, and both were half buried under newspapers and scraps and sheets of manuscript. There was a wooden box of sand, sprinkled with cigar stubs and "old soldiers," and a stove with a door hanging by its upper hinge. The chief editor had a long-tailed black cloth frock-coat on, and white linen pants. His boots were small and neatly blacked. He wore a ruffled shirt, a large seal-ring, a standing collar of obsolete pattern, and a checkered neckerchief with the ends hanging down. Date of costume about 1848. He was smoking a cigar, and trying to think of a word, and in pawing his hair he rumpled his locks a good deal. He was scowling fearfully, and I judged that he was concocting a particularly knotty editorial. He told me to take the exchanges and skim through them and write up the "Spirit of the Tennessee Press," condensing into the article all of their contents that seemed of interest.

I wrote as follows:

SPIRIT OF THE TENNESSEE PRESS

The editors of the Semi-Weekly Earthquake *evidently labor under a misapprehension with regard to the Ballyhack railroad. It is not the object of the company to leave Buzzardville off to one side. On the contrary, they consider it one of the most important points along the line, and consequently can have no desire to slight it. The gentlemen of the* Earthquake *will, of course, take pleasure in making the correction.*

John W. Blossom, Esq., the able editor of the Higginsville Thunderbolt and Battle Cry of Freedom, *arrived in the city yesterday. He is stopping at the Van Buren House.*

We observe that our contemporary of the Mud Springs Morning Howl *has fallen into the error of supposing that the election of Van Werter is not an established fact, but he will have discovered his mistake before this reminder reaches him, no doubt. He was doubtless misled by incomplete election returns.*

It is pleasant to note that the city of Blathersville is endeavoring to contract with some New York gentlemen to pave its well-nigh impassable streets with the Nicholson pavement. The Daily Hurrah *urges the measure with ability, and seems confident of ultimate success.*

I passed my manuscript over to the chief editor for acceptance, alteration, or destruction. He glanced at it and his face clouded. He ran his eye down the pages, and his countenance grew portentous. It was easy to see that something was wrong. Presently he sprang up and said:

"Thunder and lighting! Do you suppose I am going to speak of those cattle that way? Do you suppose my subscribers are going to stand such gruel as that? Give me the pen!"

I never saw a pen scrape and scratch its way so viciously, or plow through another man's verbs and adjectives so relentlessly. While he was in the midst of his work, somebody shot at him through the open window, and marred the symmetry of my ear.

"Ah," said he, "that is that scoundrel Smith, of the *Moral Volcano*—he was due yesterday." And he snatched a navy revolver from his belt and fired. Smith dropped, shot in the thigh. The shot spoiled Smith's aim, who was just taking a second chance, and he crippled a stranger. It was me. Merely a finger shot off.

Then the chief editor went on with his erasures and interlineations. Just as he finished then a hand-grenade came down the stove-pipe, and the explosion shivered the stove into a thousand fragments. However, it did no further damage, except that a vagrant piece knocked a couple of my teeth out.

"That stove is utterly ruined," said the chief editor.

I said I believed it was.

"Well, no matter—don't want it this kind of weather. I know the man that did it. I'll get him. Now, *here* is the way this stuff ought to be written."

I took the manuscript. It was scarred with erasures and interlineations till its mother wouldn't have known it if it had had one. It now read as follows:

SPIRIT OF THE TENNESSEE PRESS

The inveterate liars of the Semi-Weekly Earthquake *are evidently endeavoring to palm off upon a noble and chivalrous people another of their vile and brutal falsehoods with regard to that most glorious conception of the nineteenth century, the Ballyhack railroad. The idea that Buzzardville was to be left off at one side originated in their own fulsome brains—or rather in the settlings which they regard as brains. They had better swallow this lie if they want to save their abandoned reptile carcasses the cowhiding they so richly deserve.*

That ass, Blossom, of the Higginsville Thunderbolt and Battle Cry of Freedom, *is down here again sponging at the Van Buren.*

We observe that the besotted blackguard of the Mud Springs Morning Howl *is giving out, with his usual prosperity for lying, that Van Werter is not elected. The heaven-born mission of journalism is to disseminate truth; to eradicate error; to educate, refine, and elevate the tone of public morals and manners, and make all men more gentle, more virtuous, more charitable, and in all ways better, and holier, and happier; and yet this black-hearted scoundrel degrades his great office persistently to the dissemination of falsehood, calumny, vituperation, and vulgarity.*

Blathersville wants a Nicholson pavement—it wants a jail and a poorhouse more. The idea of a pavement in a one-horse town composed of two gin-mills, a blacksmith shop, and that mustard-plaster of a newspaper, the Daily Hurrah! *The crawling insect, Buckner, who edits the* Hurrah, *is braying about his business with his customary imbecility, and imagining he is talking sense.*

"Now *that* is the way to write—peppery and to the point. Mush-and-milk journalism gives me the fan-tods."

About this time a brick came through the window with a splintering crash, and gave me a considerable of a jolt in the back. I moved out of range—I began to feel in the way.

The chief said, "That was the Colonel, likely. I've been expecting him for two days. He will be up now right away."

He was correct. The Colonel appeared in the door a moment afterward with a dragoon revolver in his hand.

He said, "Sir, have I the honor of addressing the poltroon who edits this mangy sheet?"

"You have. Be seated, sir. Be careful of the chair, one of its legs is gone. I believe I have the honor of addressing the putrid liar, Colonel Blatherskite Tecumesh?"

"Right, sir. I have a little account to settle with you. If you are at leisure we will begin."

"I have an article on the 'Encouraging Progress of Moral and Intellectual Development in America' to finish, but there is no hurry. Begin."

Both pistols rang out their fierce clamor at the same instant. The chief lost a lock of his hair, and the Colonel's bullet ended its career in the fleshy part of my thigh. The Colonel's left shoulder was clipped a little. They fired again. Both missed their men this time, but I got my share, a shot in the arm. At the third fire both gentlemen were wounded slightly, and I had a knuckle chipped. I then said, I believed I would go out and take a walk, as this was a private matter, and I had a delicacy about participating in it further. But both gentlemen begged me to keep my seat, and assured me that I was not in the way.

They then talked about the elections and the crops while they reloaded, and I fell to tying up my wounds. But presently they opened fire again with animation, and every shot took effect—but it is proper to remark that five out of the six fell to my share. The sixth one mortally wounded the Colonel, who remarked, with fine humor, that he would have to say good morning now, as he had business uptown. He then inquired the way to the undertaker's and left.

The chief turned to me and said, "I am expecting company to dinner, and shall have to get ready. It will be a favor to me if you will read proof and attend to the customers."

I winced a little at the idea of attending to the customers, but I was too bewildered by the fusillade that was still ringing in my ears to think of anything to say.

He continued, "Jones will be here at three—cowhide him. Gillespie will call earlier, perhaps—throw him out of the window. Ferguson will be along about four—kill him. That is all for to-day, I believe. If you have any odd time, you may write a blistering article on the police—give the chief inspector rats. The cowhides are under the table; weapons in the drawer—ammunition there in the corner—lint and bandages up there in the pigeonholes. In case of accident, go to Lancet, the surgeon, down-stairs. He advertises—we take it out in trade."

He was gone. I shuddered. At the end of the next three hours I had been through perils so awful that all peace of mind and all cheerfulness were gone from me. Gillespie had called and thrown *me* out of the window. Jones arrived promptly, and when I got ready to do the cowhiding he took the job off my hands. In an encounter with a stranger, not in the bill of fare, I had lost my scalp. Another stranger, by the name of Thompson, left me a mere wreck and ruin of chaotic rags. And at last, at bay in the corner, and beset by an infuriated mob of editors, blacklegs, politicians, and desperadoes, who raved and swore and flourished their weapons about my head till the air shimmered with glancing flashes of steel, I was in the act of resigning my berth on the paper when the chief arrived, and with him a rabble of charmed and enthusiastic friends. Then ensued a scene of riot and carnage such as no human pen, or steel one either, could describe. People were shot, probed, dismembered, blown up, thrown out of the window. There was a brief tornado of murky blasphemy, with a confused and frantic war-dance glimmering through it, and then all was over. In five minutes there was silence, and the gory chief and I sat alone and surveyed the sanguinary ruin that strewed the floor around us.

He said, "You'll like this place when you get used to it."

I said, "I'll have to get you to excuse me; I think maybe I might write to suit you after a while; as soon as I had had some practice and learned the language I am confident I could. But, to speak the plain truth, that sort of energy of expression has its inconveniences, and a man is liable to interruption. You see that yourself. Vigorous writing is calculated to elevate the public, no doubt, but then I do not like to attract so much attention as it calls forth. I can't write with comfort when I am interrupted so much as I have been to-day. I like this berth well enough, but I don't like to be left here to wait on the customers. The experiences are novel, I grant you, and entertaining, too, after a fashion, but they are not judiciously distributed. A gentleman shoots at you through the window and cripples *me;* a bombshell comes down the stove-pipe for your gratification and sends the stove door down *my* throat; a friend drops in to swap compliments with you, and freckles *me* with bullet-holes till my skin won't hold my principles; you go to dinner, and Jones comes with his cowhide, Gillespie throws me out of the window, Thompson tears all my clothes off, and an entire stranger takes my scalp with the easy freedom of an old acquaintance; and in less than five minutes all the blackguards in the country arrive in their warpaint, and proceed to scare the rest of me to death with their tomahawks. Take it altogether, I never had such a spirited time in all my life as I have had to-day. No; I like you, and I like your calm unruffled way of explaining things to the customers, but you see I am not used to it. The Southern heart is too impulsive; Southern hospitality is too lavish with the stranger. The paragraphs which I have written to-day, and into whose cold sentences your masterly hand has infused the fervent spirit of Tennesseean journalism, will wake up another nest of hornets. All that mob of editors will come—and they will come hungry, too, and want somebody for breakfast. I shall have to bid you adieu. I decline to be present at these festivities. I came South for my health, I will go back on the same errand, and suddenly. Tennesseean journalism is too stirring for me."

After which we parted with mutual regret, and I took apartments at the hospital.

1869

How I Edited an Agricultural Paper

I did not take temporary editorship of an agricultural paper without misgivings. Neither would a landsman take command of a ship without misgivings. But I was in circumstances that made the salary an object. The regular editor of the paper was going off for a holiday, and I accepted the terms he offered, and took his place.

The sensation of being at work again was luxurious, and I wrought all the week with unflagging pleasure. We went to press, and I waited a day with some solicitude to see whether my effort was going to attract any notice. As I left the office, toward sundown, a group of men and boys at the foot of the stairs dispersed with one impulse, and gave me passageway, and I heard one or two of them say: "That's him!" I was naturally pleased by this incident. The next morning I found a similar group at the foot of the stairs, and scattering couples and individuals standing here and there in the street and over the way, watching me with interest. The group separated and fell back as I approached, and I heard a man say, "Look at his eye!" I pretended not to observe the notice I was attracting, but secretly I was pleased with it, and was purposing to write an account of it to my aunt. I went up the short flight of stairs, and heard cheery voices and a ringing laugh as I drew near the door, which I opened, and caught a glimpse of two young rural-looking men, whose faces blanched and lengthened when they saw me, and then they both plunged through the window with a great crash. I was surprised.

In about half an hour an old gentleman, with a flowing beard and a fine but rather austere face, entered, and sat down at my invitation. He seemed to have something on his mind. He took off his hat and set it on the floor, and got out of it a red silk handkerchief and a copy of our paper.

He put the paper on his lap, and while he polished his spectacles with his handkerchief he said, "Are you the new editor?"

I said I was.

"Have you ever edited an agricultural paper before?"

"No," I said; "this is my first attempt."

"Very likely. Have you had any experience in agriculture practically?"

"No; I believe I have not."

"Some instinct told me so," said the old gentleman, putting on his spectacles, and looking over them at me with asperity, while he folded his paper into a convenient shape. "I wish to read you what must have made me have that instinct. It was this editorial. Listen, and see if it was you that wrote it:

"'*Turnips should never be pulled, it injures them. It is much better to send a boy up and let him shake the tree.*'

"Now, what do you think of that?—for I really suppose you wrote it?"

"Think of it? Why, I think it is good. I think it is sense. I have no doubt that every year millions and millions of bushels of turnips are spoiled in this township alone by being pulled in a half-ripe condition, when, if they had sent a boy up to shake the tree—"

"Shake your grandmother! Turnips don't grow on trees!"

"Oh, they don't, don't they? Well, who said they did? The language was intended to be figurative, wholly figurative. Anybody that knows anything will know that I meant that the boy should shake the vine."

Then this old person got up and tore his paper all into small shreds, and stamped on them, and broke several things with his cane, and said I did not know as much as a cow; and then went out and banged the door after him, and, in short, acted in such a way that I fancied he was displeased about something. But not knowing what the trouble was, I could not be any help to him.

Pretty soon after this a long, cadaverous creature, with lanky locks hanging down to his shoulders, and a week's stubble bristling from the hills and valleys of his face, darted within the door, and halted, motionless, with finger on lip, and head and body bent in listening attitude. No sound was heard. Still he listened. No sound. Then he turned the key in the door, and came elaborately tiptoeing toward me till he was within long reaching distance of me, when he stopped and, after scanning my face with intense interest for a while, drew a folded copy of our paper from his bosom, and said:

"There, you wrote that. Read it to me—quick! Relieve me. I suffer."

I read as follows; and as the sentences fell from my lips I could see the relief come, I could see the drawn muscles relax, and the anxiety go out of the face, and rest and peace steal over the features like the merciful moonlight over a desolate landscape:

The guano is a fine bird, but great care is necessary in rearing it. It should not be imported earlier than June or later than September. In the winter it should be kept in a warm place, where it can hatch out its young.

It is evident that we are to have a backward season for grain. Therefore it will be well for the farmer to begin setting out his corn-stalks and planting his buckwheat cakes in July instead of August.

Concerning the pumpkin. This berry is a favorite with the natives of the interior of New England, who prefer it to the gooseberry for the making of fruit-cake, and who likewise give it the preference over the raspberry for feeding cows, as being more filling and fully as satisfying. The pumpkin is the only esculent of the orange family that will thrive in the North, except the gourd and one or two varieties of the squash. But the custom of planting it in the front yard with the shrubbery is fast going out of vogue, for it is now generally conceded that the pumpkin as a shade tree is a failure.

Now, as the warm weather approaches, and the ganders begin to spawn—

The excited listener sprang toward me to shake hands, and said:

"There, there—that will do. I know I am all right now, because you have read it just as I did, word for word. But, stranger, when I first read it this morning, I said to myself, I never, never believed it before, notwithstanding my friends kept me under watch so strict, but now I believe I *am* crazy; and with that I fetched a howl that you might have heard two miles, and started out to kill somebody—because, you know, I knew it would come to that sooner or later, and so I might as well begin. I read one of them paragraphs over again, so as to be certain, and then I burned my house down and started. I have crippled several people, and have got one fellow up a tree, where I can get him if I want him. But I thought I would call in here as I passed along and make the thing perfectly certain; and now it *is* certain, and I tell you it is lucky for the chap that is in the tree. I should have killed him sure, as I went back. Good-by, sir, good-by; you have taken a great load off my mind. My reason has stood the strain of one of your agricultural articles, and I know that nothing can ever unseat it now. *Good*-by, sir."

I felt a little uncomfortable about the cripplings and arsons this person had been entertaining himself with, for I could not help feeling remotely accessory to them. But these thoughts were quickly banished, for the regular editor walked in! [I thought to myself, Now if you had gone to Egypt as I recommended you to, I might have had a chance to get my hand in; but you wouldn't do it, and here you are. I sort of expected you.]

The editor was looking sad and perplexed and dejected.

He surveyed the wreck which that old rioter and those two young farmers had made, and then said: "This is a sad business—a very sad business. There is the mucilage-bottle broken, and six panes of glass, and a spittoon, and two candlesticks. But that is not the worst. The reputation of the paper is injured—and permanently, I fear. True, there never was such a call for the paper before, and it never sold such a large edition or soared to such celebrity;—but does one want to be famous for lunacy, and prosper upon the infirmities of his mind? My friend, as I am an honest man, the street out here is full of people, and others are roosting on the fences, waiting to get a glimpse of you, because they think you are crazy. And well they might after reading your editorials. They are a disgrace to journalism. Why, what put it into your head that you could edit a paper of this nature? You do not seem to know the first rudiments of agriculture. You speak of a furrow and a harrow as being the same thing; you talk of the moulting season for cows; and you recommend the domestication of the pole-cat on account of its playfulness and its excellence as a ratter! Your remark that clams will lie quiet if music be played to them was superfluous—entirely superfluous. Nothing disturbs clams. Clams *always* lie quiet. Clams care nothing whatever about music. Ah, heavens and earth, friend! if you had made the acquiring of ignorance the study of your life, you could not have graduated with higher honor than you could to-day. I never saw anything like it. Your observation that the horse-chestnut as an article of commerce is steadily gaining in favor is simply calculated to destroy this journal. I want you to throw up your situation and go. I want no more holiday—I could not enjoy it if I had it. Certainly not with you in my chair. I would always stand in dread of what you might be going to recommend next. It makes me lose all patience every time I think of your discussing oyster-beds under the head of 'Landscape Gardening.' I want you to go. Nothing on earth could persuade me to take another holiday. Oh! why didn't you *tell* me you didn't know anything about agriculture?"

"*Tell* you, you corn-stalk, you cabbage, you son of a cauliflower? It's the first time I ever heard such an unfeeling remark. I tell you I have been in the editorial business going on fourteen years, and it is the first time I ever heard of a man's having to know anything in order to edit a newspaper. You turnip! Who write the dramatic critiques for the second-rate papers? Why, a parcel of promoted shoemakers and apprentice apothecaries, who know just as much about good acting as I do about good farming and no more. Who review the books? People who never wrote one. Who do up the heavy leaders on finance? Parties who have had the largest opportunities for knowing nothing about it. Who criticize the Indian campaigns? Gentlemen who do not know a war-whoop from a wigwam, and who never have had to run a foot-race with a tomahawk, or pluck arrows out of the several members of their families to build the evening camp-fire with. Who write the temperance appeals, and clamor about the flowing bowl? Folks who will never draw another sober breath till they do it in the grave. Who edit the agricultural papers, you—yam? Men, as a general thing, who fail in the poetry line, yellow-colored novel line, sensation-drama line, city-editor line, and finally fall back on agriculture as a temporary reprieve from the poor-house. *You* try to tell *me* anything about the newspaper business! Sir, I have been through it from Alpha to Omaha, and I tell you that the less a man knows the bigger the noise he makes and the higher the salary he commands. Heaven knows if I had but been ignorant instead of cultivated, and impudent instead of diffident, I could have made a name for myself in this cold, selfish world. I take my leave, sir. Since I have been treated as you have treated me, I am perfectly willing to go. But I have done my duty. I have fulfilled my contract as far as I was permitted to do it. I said I could make your paper of interest to all classes—and I have. I said I could run your circulation up to twenty thousand copies, and if I had had two more weeks I'd have done it. And I'd have given you the best class of readers that ever an agricultural paper had—not a farmer in it, nor a solitary individual who could tell a watermelon-tree from a peach-vine to save his life. *You* are the loser by this rupture, not me, Pie-plant. *Adios.*"

I then left.

1870

The Stolen White Elephant*

1

The following curious history was related to me by a chance railway acquaintance. He was a gentleman more than seventy years of age, and his thoroughly good and gentle face and earnest and sincere manner imprinted the unmistakable stamp of truth upon every statement which fell from his lips. He said:

You know in what reverence the royal white elephant of Siam is held by the people of that country. You know it is sacred to kings, only kings may possess it, and that it is, indeed, in a measure even superior to kings, since it receives not merely honor but worship. Very well; five years ago, when the troubles concerning the frontier line arose between Great Britain and Siam, it was presently manifest that Siam had been in the wrong. Therefore every reparation was quickly made, and the British representative stated that he was satisfied and the past should be forgotten. This greatly relieved the King of Siam, and partly as a token of gratitude, but partly also, perhaps, to wipe out any little remaining vestige of unpleasantness which England might feel toward him, he wished to send the Queen a present—the sole sure way of propitiating an enemy, according to Oriental ideas. This present ought not only to be a royal one, but transcendently

* Left out of *A Tramp Abroad*, because it was feared that some of the particulars had been exaggerated, and that others were not true. Before these suspicions had been proven groundless, the book had gone to press. M.T.

royal. Wherefore, what offering could be so meet as that of a white elephant? My position in the Indian civil service was such that I was deemed peculiarly worthy of the honor of conveying the present to her Majesty. A ship was fitted out for me and my servants and the officers and attendants of the elephant, and in due time I arrived in New York harbor and placed my royal charge in admirable quarters in Jersey City. It was necessary to remain awhile in order to recruit the animal's health before resuming the voyage.

All went well during a fortnight—then my calamities began. The white elephant was stolen! I was called up at dead of night and informed of this fearful misfortune. For some moments I was beside myself with terror and anxiety; I was helpless. Then I grew calmer and collected my faculties. I soon saw my course—for, indeed, there was but the one course for an intelligent man to pursue. Late as it was, I flew to New York and got a policeman to conduct me to the headquarters of the detective force. Fortunately I arrived in time, though the chief of the force, the celebrated Inspector Blunt, was just on the point of leaving for his home. He was a man of middle size and compact frame, and when he was thinking deeply he had a way of knitting his brows and tapping his forehead reflectively with his finger, which impressed you at once with the conviction that you stood in the presence of a person of no common order. The very sight of him gave me confidence and made me hopeful. I stated my errand. It did not flurry him in the least; it had no more visible effect upon his iron self-possession than if I had told him somebody had stolen my dog. He motioned me to a seat, and said, calmly:

"Allow me to think a moment, please."

So saying, he sat down at his office table and leaned his head upon his hand. Several clerks were at work at the other end of the room; the scratching of their pens was all the sound I heard during the next six or seven minutes. Meantime the inspector sat there, buried in thought. Finally he raised his head, and there was that in the firm lines of his face which showed me that his brain had done its work and his plan was made. Said he—and his voice was low and impressive:

"This is no ordinary case. Every step must be warily taken; each step must be made sure before the next is ventured. And secrecy must be observed—secrecy profound and absolute. Speak to no one about the matter, not even the reporters. I will take care of *them;* I will see that they get only what it may suit my ends to let them know." He touched a bell; a youth appeared. "Alaric, tell the reporters to remain for the present." The boy retired. "Now let us proceed to business—and systematically. Nothing can be accomplished in this trade of mine without strict and minute method."

He took a pen and some paper. "Now—name of the elephant?"

"Hassan Ben Ali Ben Selim Abdallah Mohammed Moisé Al hammal Jamsetjejeebhoy Dhuleep Sultan Ebu Bhudpoor."

"Very well. Given name?"

"Jumbo."

"Very well. Place of birth?"

"The capital city of Siam."

"Parents living?"

"No—dead."

"Had they any other issue besides this one?"

"None. He was an only child."

"Very well. These matters are sufficient under that head. Now please describe the elephant, and leave out no particular, however insignificant—that is, insignificant from *your* point of view. To men in my profession there *are* no insignificant particulars; they do not exist."

I described—he wrote. When I was done, he said:

"Now listen. If I have made any mistakes, correct me."

He read as follows:

"Height, 19 feet; length from apex of forehead to insertion of tail, 26 feet; length of trunk, 16 feet; length of tail, 6 feet; total length, including trunk and tail, 48 feet; length of tusks, 91⁄2 feet; ears in keeping with these dimensions; footprint resembles the mark left when one upends a barrel in the snow; color of the elephant, a dull white; has a hole the size of a plate in each ear for the insertion of jewelry, and possesses the habit in a remarkable degree of squirting water upon spectators and of maltreating with his trunk not only such persons as he is acquainted with, but even entire strangers; limps slightly with his right hind leg, and has a small scar in his left armpit caused by a former boil; had on, when stolen, a castle containing seats for fifteen persons, and a gold-cloth saddle-blanket the size of an ordinary carpet."

There were no mistakes. The inspector touched the bell, handed the description to Alaric, and said:

"Have fifty thousand copies of this printed at once and mailed to every detective office and pawnbroker's shop on the continent." Alaric retired. "There—so far, so good. Next, I must have a photograph of the property."

I gave him one. He examined it critically, and said:

"It must do, since we can do no better; but he has his trunk curled up and tucked into his mouth. That is unfortunate, and is calculated to mislead, for of course he does not usually have it in that position." He touched his bell.

"Alaric, have fifty thousand copies of this photograph made the first thing in the morning, and mail them with the descriptive circulars."

Alaric retired to execute his orders. The inspector said:

"It will be necessary to offer a reward, of course. Now as to the amount?"

"What sum would you suggest?"

"To *begin* with, I should say—well, twenty-five thousand dollars. It is an intricate and difficult business; there are a thousand avenues of escape and opportunities of concealment. These thieves have friends and pals everywhere—"

"Bless me, do you know who they are?"

The wary face, practised in concealing the thoughts and feelings within, gave me no token, nor yet the replying words, so quietly uttered:

"Never mind about that. I may, and I may not. We generally gather a pretty shrewd inkling of who our man is by the manner of his work and the size of the game he goes after. We are not dealing with a pickpocket or a hall thief now, make up your mind to that. This property was not 'lifted' by a novice. But, as I was saying, considering the amount of travel which will have to be done, and the diligence with which the thieves will cover up their traces as they move along, twenty-five thousand may be too small a sum to offer, yet I think it worth while to start with that."

So we determined upon that figure as a beginning. Then this man, whom nothing escaped which could by any possibility be made to serve as a clue, said:

"There are cases in detective history to show that criminals have been detected through peculiarities in their appetites. Now, what does this elephant eat, and how much?"

"Well, as to *what* he eats—he will eat *anything*. He will eat a man, he will eat a Bible—he will eat anything *between* a man and a Bible."

"Good—very good, indeed, but too general. Details are necessary—details are the only valuable things in our trade. Very well—as to men. At one meal—or, if you prefer, during one day—how many men will he eat, if fresh?"

"He would not care whether they were fresh or not; at a single meal he would eat five ordinary men."

"Very good; five men; we will put that down. What nationalities would he prefer?"

"He is indifferent about nationalities. He prefers acquaintances, but is not prejudiced against strangers."

"Very good. Now, as to Bibles. How many Bibles would he eat at a meal?"

"He would eat an entire edition."

"It is hardly succinct enough. Do you mean the ordinary octavo, or the family illustrated?"

"I think he would be indifferent to illustrations; that is, I think he would not value illustrations above simple letter-press."

"No, you do not get my idea. I refer to bulk. The ordinary octavo Bible weighs about two pounds and a half, while the great quarto with the illustrations weighs ten or twelve. How many Doré Bibles would he eat at a meal?"

"If you knew this elephant, you could not ask. He would take what they had."

"Well, put it in dollars and cents, then. We must get at it somehow. The Doré costs a hundred dollars a copy, Russia leather, beveled."

"He would require about fifty thousand dollars' worth—say an edition of five hundred copies."

"Now that is more exact. I will put that down. Very well; he likes men and Bibles; so far, so good. What else will he eat? I want particulars."

"He will leave Bibles to eat bricks, he will leave bricks to eat bottles, he will leave bottles to eat clothing, he will leave clothing to eat cats, he will leave cats to eat oysters, he will leave oysters to eat ham, he will leave ham to eat sugar, he will leave sugar to eat pie, he will leave pie to eat potatoes, he will leave potatoes to eat bran, he will leave bran to eat hay, he will leave hay to eat oats, he will leave oats to eat rice, for he was mainly raised on it. There is nothing whatever that he will not eat but European butter, and he would eat that if he could taste it."

"Very good. General quantity at a meal—say about—"

"Well, anywhere from a quarter to half a ton."

"And he drinks—"

"Everything that is fluid. Milk, water, whisky, molasses, castor oil, camphene, carbolic acid—it is no use to go into particulars; whatever fluid occurs to you set it down. He will drink anything that is fluid, except European coffee."

"Very good. As to quantity?"

"Put it down five to fifteen barrels—his thirst varies; his other appetites do not."

"These things are unusual. They ought to furnish quite good clues toward tracing him."

He touched the bell.

"Alaric, summon Captain Burns."

Burns appeared. Inspector Blunt unfolded the whole matter to him, detail by detail. Then he said in the clear, decisive tones of a man whose plans are clearly defined in his head and who is accustomed to command:

"Captain Burns, detail Detectives Jones, Davis, Halsey, Bates, and Hackett to shadow the elephant."

"Yes, sir."

"Detail Detectives Moses, Dakin, Murphy, Rogers, Tupper, Higgins, and Bartholomew to shadow the thieves."

"Yes, sir."

"Place a strong guard—a guard of thirty picked men, with a relief of thirty—over the place from whence the elephant was stolen, to keep strict watch there night and day, and allow none to approach—except reporters—without written authority from me."

"Yes, sir."

"Place detectives in plain clothes in the railway, steamship, and ferry depots, and upon all roadways leading out of Jersey City, with orders to search all suspicious persons."

"Yes, sir."

"Furnish all these men with photograph and accompanying description of the elephant, and instruct them to search all trains and outgoing ferryboats and other vessels."

"Yes, sir."

"If the elephant should be found, let him be seized, and the information forwarded to me by telegraph."

"Yes, sir."

"Let me be informed at once if any clues should be found—footprints of the animal, or anything of that kind."

"Yes, sir."

"Get an order commanding the harbor police to patrol the frontages vigilantly."

"Yes, sir."

"Despatch detectives in plain clothes over all the railways, north as far as Canada, west as far as Ohio, south as far as Washington."

"Yes, sir."

"Place experts in all the telegraph offices to listen to all messages; and let them require that all cipher despatches be interpreted to them."

"Yes, sir."

"Let all these things be done with the utmost secrecy—mind, the most impenetrable secrecy."

"Yes, sir."

"Report to me promptly at the usual hour."

"Yes, sir."

"Go!"

"Yes, sir."

He was gone.

Inspector Blunt was silent and thoughtful a moment, while the fire in his eye cooled down and faded out. Then he turned to me and said in a placid voice:

"I am not given to boasting, it is not my habit; but—we shall find the elephant."

I shook him warmly by the hand and thanked him; and I *felt* my thanks, too. The more I had seen of the man the more I liked him and the more I admired him and marveled over the mysterious wonders of his profession. Then we parted for the night, and I went home with a far happier heart than I had carried with me to his office.

2

Next morning it was all in the newspapers, in the minutest detail. It even had additions—consisting of Detective This, Detective That, and Detective The Other's "Theory" as to how the robbery was done, who the robbers were, and whither they had flown with their booty. There were eleven of these theories, and they covered all the possibilities; and this single fact shows what independent thinkers detectives are. No two theories were alike, or even much resembled each other, save in one striking particular, and in that one all the other eleven theories were absolutely agreed. That was, that although the rear of my building was torn out and the only door remained locked, the elephant had not been removed through the rent, but by some other (undiscovered) outlet. All agreed that the robbers had made that rent only to mislead the detectives. That never would have occurred to me or to any other layman, perhaps, but it had not deceived the detectives for a moment. Thus, what I had supposed was the only thing that had no mystery about it was in fact the very thing I had gone furthest astray in. The eleven theories all named the supposed robbers, but no two named the same robbers; the total number of suspected persons was thirty-seven. The various newspaper accounts all closed with the most important opinion of all—that of Chief Inspector Blunt. A portion of this statement read as follows:

The chief knows who the two principals are, namely, "Brick" Duffy and "Red" McFadden. Ten days before the robbery was achieved he was already aware that it was to be attempted, and had quietly proceeded to shadow these two noted villains; but unfortunately on the night in question their track was lost, and before it could be found again the bird was flown—that is, the elephant.

Duffy and McFadden are the boldest scoundrels in the profession; the chief has reasons for believing that they are the men who stole the stove out of the detective headquarters on a bitter night last winter—in consequence of which the chief and every detective present were in the hands of the physicians before morning, some with frozen feet, others with frozen fingers, ears, and other members.

When I read the first half of that I was more astonished than ever at the wonderful sagacity of this strange man. He not only saw everything in the present with a clear eye, but even the future could not be hidden from him. I was soon at his office, and said I could not help wishing he had had those men arrested, and so prevented the trouble and loss; but his reply was simple and unanswerable:

"It is not our province to prevent crime, but to punish it. We cannot punish it until it is committed."

I remarked that the secrecy with which he had begun had been marred by the newspapers; not only all our facts but all our plans and purposes had been revealed; even all the suspected persons had been named; these would doubtless disguise themselves now, or go into hiding.

"Let them. They will find that when I am ready for them my hand will descend upon them, in their secret places, as unerringly as the hand of fate. As to the newspapers, we *must* keep in with them. Fame, reputation, constant public mention—these are the detective's bread and butter. He must publish his facts, else he will be supposed to have none; he must publish his theory, for nothing is so strange or striking as a detective's theory, or brings him so much wonderful respect; we must publish our plans, for these the journals insist upon having, and we could not deny them without offending. We must constantly show the public what we are doing, or they will believe we are doing nothing. It is much pleasanter to have a newspaper say, 'Inspector Blunt's ingenious and extraordinary theory is as follows,' than to have it say some harsh thing, or, worse still, some sarcastic one."

"I see the force of what you say. But I noticed that in one part of your remarks in the papers this morning you refused to reveal your opinion upon a certain minor point."

"Yes, we always do that; it has a good effect. Besides, I had not formed any opinion on that point, anyway."

I deposited a considerable sum of money with the inspector, to meet current expenses, and sat down to wait for news. We were expecting the telegrams to begin to arrive at any moment now. Meantime I reread the newspapers and also our descriptive circular, and observed that our twenty-five thousand dollars' reward seemed to be offered only to detectives. I said I thought it ought to be offered to anybody who would catch the elephant. The inspector said:

"It is the detectives who will find the elephant, hence the reward will go to the right place. If other people found the animal, it would only be by watching the detectives and taking advantage of clues and indications stolen from them, and that would entitle the detectives to the reward, after all. The proper office of a reward is to stimulate the men who deliver up their time and their trained sagacities to this sort of work, and not to confer benefits, upon chance citizens who stumble upon a capture without having earned the benefits by their own merits and labors."

This was reasonable enough, certainly. Now the telegraphic machine in the corner began to click, and the following despatch was the result:

FLOWER STATION, N. Y., 7.30 A.M.

HAVE GOT A CLUE. FOUND A SUCCESSION OF DEEP TRACKS ACROSS A FARM NEAR HERE. FOLLOWED THEM TWO MILES EAST WITHOUT RESULT; THINK ELEPHANT WENT WEST. SHALL NOW SHADOW HIM IN THAT DIRECTION. . . . .

DARLEY, DETECTIVE

"Darley's one of the best men on the force," said the inspector. "We shall hear from him again before long."

Telegram No. 2 came:

BARKER'S, N. J., 7.40 A.M.

JUST ARRIVED. GLASS FACTORY BROKEN OPEN HERE DURING NIGHT, AND EIGHT HUNDRED BOTTLES TAKEN. ONLY WATER IN LARGE QUANTITY NEAR HERE IS FIVE MILES DISTANT. SHALL STRIKE FOR THERE. ELEPHANT

WILL BE THIRSTY. BOTTLES WERE EMPTY.

BAKER, DETECTIVE

"That promises well, too," said the inspector. "I told you the creature's appetites would not be bad clues."

Telegram No. 3:

TAYLORVILLE, L. I., 8.15 A.M.

A HAYSTACK NEAR HERE DISAPPEARED DURING NIGHT. PROBABLY EATEN. HAVE GOT A CLUE, AND AM OFF.

HUBBARD, DETECTIVE

"How he does move around!" said the inspector. "I knew we had a difficult job on hand, but we shall catch him yet."

FLOWER STATION, N.Y., 9 A.M.

SHADOWED THE TRACKS THREE MILES WESTWARD. LARGE, DEEP AND RAGGED. HAVE JUST MET A FARMER WHO SAYS THEY ARE NOT ELEPHANT TRACKS. SAYS THEY ARE HOLES WHERE HE DUG UP SAPLINGS FOR SHADE-TREES WHEN GROUND WAS FROZEN LAST WINTER. GIVE ME ORDERS HOW TO PROCEED.

DARLEY, DETECTIVE

"Aha! a confederate of the thieves! The thing grows warm," said the inspector.

He dictated the following telegram to Darley:

ARREST THE MAN AND FORCE HIM TO NAME HIS PALS. CONTINUE TO FOLLOW THE TRACKS—TO THE PACIFIC IF NECESSARY.

CHIEF BLUNT

Next telegram:

CONEY POINT, PA., 8.45 A.M.

GAS OFFICE BROKEN OPEN HERE DURING NIGHT AND THREE MONTHS' UNPAID GAS BILLS TAKEN. HAVE GOT A CLUE AND AM AWAY.

MURPHY, DETECTIVE

"Heavens!" said the inspector; "would he eat gas bills?"

"Through ignorance—yes; but they cannot support life. At least, unassisted."

Now came this exciting telegram:

IRONVILLE, N. Y., 9.30 A.M.

JUST ARRIVED. THIS VILLAGE IN CONSTERNATION. ELEPHANT PASSED THROUGH HERE AT FIVE THIS MORNING. SOME SAY HE WENT EAST, SOME SAY WEST, SOME NORTH, SOME SOUTH—BUT ALL SAY THEY DID NOT WAIT TO NOTICE PARTICULARLY. HE KILLED A HORSE; HAVE SECURED A PIECE OF IT FOR A CLUE. KILLED IT WITH HIS TRUNK; FROM STYLE OF BLOW, THINK HE STRUCK IT LEFT-HANDED. FROM POSITION IN WHICH HORSE LIES, THINK ELEPHANT TRAVELED NORTHWARD ALONG LINE OF BERKLEY RAILWAY. HAS FOUR AND A HALF HOURS' START, BUT I MOVE ON HIS TRACK AT ONCE.

HAWES, DETECTIVE

I uttered exclamations of joy. The inspector was as self-contained as a graven image. He calmly touched his bell.

"Alaric, send Captain Burns here."

Burns appeared.

"How many men are ready for instant orders?"

"Ninety-six, sir."

"Send them north at once. Let them concentrate along the line of the Berkley road north of Ironville."

"Yes, sir."

"Let them conduct their movements with the utmost secrecy. As fast as others are at liberty, hold them for orders."

"Yes, sir."

"Go!"

"Yes, sir."

Presently came another telegram:

SAGE CORNERS, N. Y., 10.30.

JUST ARRIVED, ELEPHANT PASSED THROUGH HERE AT 8.15. ALL ESCAPED FROM THE TOWN BUT A POLICEMAN. APPARENTLY ELEPHANT DID NOT STRIKE AT POLICEMAN, BUT AT THE LAMPPOST. GOT BOTH. I HAVE SECURED A PORTION OF THE POLICEMAN AS CLUE.

STUMM, DETECTIVE

"So the elephant has turned westward," said the inspector. "However, he will not escape, for my men are scattered all over that region."

The next telegram said:

GLOVER'S, 11.15.

JUST ARRIVED. VILLAGE DESERTED, EXCEPT SICK AND AGED. ELEPHANT PASSED THROUGH THREE-QUARTERS OF AN HOUR AGO. THE ANTITEMPERANCE MASS-MEETING WAS IN SESSION; HE PUT HIS TRUNK IN AT A WINDOW AND WASHED IT OUT WITH WATER FROM CISTERN. SOME SWALLOWED IT—SINCE DEAD; SEVERAL DROWNED. DETECTIVES CROSS AND O'SHAUGHNESSY WERE PASSING

THROUGH TOWN, BUT GOING SOUTH—SO MISSED ELEPHANT. WHOLE REGION FOR MANY MILES AROUND IN TERROR—PEOPLE FLYING FROM THEIR HOMES. WHEREVER THEY TURN MEET ELEPHANT, AND MANY ARE KILLED.

BRANT, DETECTIVE

I could have shed tears, this havoc so distressed me. But the inspector only said:

"You see—we are closing in on him. He feels our presence; he has turned eastward again."

Yet further troublous news was in store for us. The telegraph brought this:

HOGANSPORT, 12.19.

JUST ARRIVED. ELEPHANT PASSED THROUGH HALF AN HOUR AGO, CREATING WILDEST FRIGHT AND EXCITEMENT. ELEPHANT RAGED AROUND STREETS: TWO PLUMBERS GOING BY, KILLED ONE.—OTHER ESCAPED. REGRET GENERAL.

O'FLAHERTY, DETECTIVE

"Now he is right in the midst of my men," said the inspector. "Nothing can save him."

A succession of telegrams came from detectives who were scattered through New Jersey and Pennsylvania, and who were following clues consisting of ravaged barns, factories, and Sunday-school libraries, with high hopes—hopes amounting to certainties, indeed. The inspector said:

"I wish I could communicate with them and order them north, but that is impossible. A detective only visits a telegraph office to send his report; then he is off again, and you don't know where to put your hand on him."

Now came this despatch:

BRIDGEPORT, CT., 12.15.

BARNUM OFFERS RATE OF $4,000 A YEAR FOR EXCLUSIVE PRIVILEGE OF USING ELEPHANT AS TRAVELING ADVERTISING MEDIUM FROM NOW TILL DETECTIVES FIND HIM. WANTS TO PASTE CIRCUS-POSTERS ON HIM. DESIRES IMMEDIATE ANSWER.

BOGGS, DETECTIVE

"That is perfectly absurd!" I exclaimed.

"Of course it is," said the inspector. "Evidently Mr. Barnum, who thinks he is so sharp, does not know me—but I know him."

Then he dictated this answer to the despatch:

MR. BARNUM'S OFFER DECLINED. MAKE IT $7,000 OR NOTHING.

CHIEF BLUNT

"There. We shall not have to wait long for an answer. Mr. Barnum is not at home; he is in the telegraph office—it is his way when he has business on hand. Inside of three—"

DONE.—P.T. BARNUM

So interrupted the clicking telegraphic instrument. Before I could make a comment upon this extraordinary episode, the following despatch carried my thoughts into another very distressing channel:

BOLIVIA, N.Y., 12.50.

ELEPHANT ARRIVED HERE FROM THE SOUTH AND PASSED THROUGH TOWARD THE FOREST AT 11.50,

DISPERSING A FUNERAL ON THE WAY, AND DIMINISHING THE MOURNERS BY TWO. CITIZENS FIRED SOME SMALL CANNON-BALLS INTO HIM, AND THEN FLED. DETECTIVE BURKE AND I ARRIVED TEN MINUTES LATER, FROM THE NORTH, BUT MISTOOK SOME EXCAVATIONS FOR FOOT-PRINTS, AND SO LOST A GOOD DEAL OF TIME; BUT AT LAST WE STRUCK THE RIGHT TRAIL AND FOLLOWED IT TO THE WOODS. WE THEN GOT DOWN ON OUR HANDS AND KNEES AND CONTINUED TO KEEP A SHARP EYE ON THE TRACK, AND SO SHADOWED IT INTO THE BRUSH. BURKE WAS IN ADVANCE. UNFORTUNATELY THE ANIMAL HAD STOPPED TO REST; THEREFORE, BURKE HAVING HIS HEAD DOWN, INTENT UPON THE TRACK, BUTTED UP AGAINST THE ELEPHANT'S HIND LEGS BEFORE HE WAS AWARE OF HIS VICINITY. BURKE INSTANTLY AROSE TO HIS FEET, SEIZED THE TAIL, AND EXCLAIMED JOYFULLY, "I CLAIM THE RE—" BUT GOT NO FURTHER, FOR A SINGLE BLOW OF THE HUGE TRUNK LAID THE BRAVE FELLOW'S FRAGMENTS LOW IN DEATH. I FLED REARWARD, AND THE ELEPHANT TURNED AND SHADOWED ME TO THE EDGE OF THE WOOD, MAKING TREMENDOUS SPEED, AND I SHOULD INEVITABLY HAVE BEEN LOST, BUT THAT THE REMAINS OF THE FUNERAL PROVIDENTIALLY INTER-VENED AGAIN AND DIVERTED HIS ATTENTION. I HAVE JUST LEARNED THAT NOTHING OF THAT FUNERAL IS NOW LEFT; BUT THIS IS NO LOSS, FOR THERE IS ABUN-DANCE OF MATERIAL FOR ANOTHER. MEANTIME, THE ELEPHANT HAS DISAPPEARED AGAIN.

MULROONEY, DETECTIVE

We heard no news except from the diligent and confident detectives scattered about New Jersey, Pennsylvania, Delaware, and

Virginia—who were all following fresh and encouraging clues—until shortly after 2 P.M., when this telegram came:

BAXTER CENTER, 2.15.

ELEPHANT BEEN HERE, PLASTERED OVER WITH CIRCUS-BILLS, AND BROKE UP A REVIVAL, STRIKING DOWN AND DAMAGING MANY WHO WERE ON THE POINT OF ENTERING UPON A BETTER LIFE. CITIZENS PENNED UP AND ESTABLISHED A GUARD. WHEN DETECTIVE BROWN AND I ARRIVED, SOME TIME AFTER, WE ENTERED INCLOSURE AND PROCEEDED TO IDENTIFY ELEPHANT BY PHOTOGRAPHS AND DESCRIPTION. ALL MARKS TALLIED EXACTLY EXCEPT ONE, WHICH WE COULD NOT SEE—THE BOIL-SCAR UNDER ARMPIT. TO MAKE SURE, BROWN CREPT UNDER TO LOOK, AND WAS IMMEDIATELY BRAINED—THAT IS, HEAD CRUSHED AND DESTROYED, THOUGH NOTHING ISSUED FROM DEBRIS. ALL FLED; SO DID ELEPHANT, STRIKING RIGHT AND LEFT WITH MUCH EFFECT. HAS ESCAPED, BUT LEFT BOLD BLOOD-TRACK FROM CANNON-WOUNDS. REDISCOVERY CERTAIN. HE BROKE SOUTHWARD, THROUGH A DENSE FOREST.

BRENT, DETECTIVE

That was the last telegram. At nightfall a fog shut down which was so dense that objects but three feet away could not be discerned. This lasted all night. The ferryboats and even the omnibuses had to stop running.

3

Next morning the papers were as full of detective theories as before; they had all our tragic facts in detail also, and a great many more which they had received from their telegraphic correspondents. Column after column was occupied, a third of its way down, with glaring head-lines, which it made my heart sick to read. Their general tone was like this:

> THE WHITE ELEPHANT AT LARGE! HE MOVES UPON HIS FATAL MARCH! WHOLE VILLAGES DESERTED BY THEIR FRIGHT-STRICKEN OCCUPANTS! PALE TERROR GOES BEFORE HIM, DEATH AND DEVASTATION FOLLOW AFTER! AFTER THESE, THE DETECTIVES! BARNS DESTROYED, FACTORIES GUTTED, HARVESTS DEVOURED, PUBLIC ASSEMBLAGES DISPERSED, ACCOMPANIED BY SCENES OF CARNAGE IMPOSSIBLE TO DESCRIBE! THEORIES OF THIRTY-FOUR OF THE MOST DISTINGUISHED DETECTIVES ON THE FORCE! THEORY OF CHIEF BLUNT!

"There!" said Inspector Blunt, almost betrayed into excitement, "this is magnificent! This is the greatest windfall that any detective organization ever had. The fame of it will travel to the ends of the earth, and endure to the end of time, and my name with it."

But there was no joy for me. I felt as if I had committed all those red crimes, and that the elephant was only my irresponsible agent. And how the list had grown! In one place he had "interfered with an election and killed five repeaters." He had followed this act with the destruction of two poor fellows, named O'Donohue and McFlannigan, who had "found a refuge in the home of the oppressed of all lands only the day before, and were in the act of exercising for the first time the noble right of American citizens at the polls, when stricken down by the relentless hand of the Scourge of Siam." In another, he had "found a crazy sensation-preacher preparing his next season's heroic attacks on the dance, the theater, and other things which can't strike back, and had stepped on him." And in still another place he had "killed a lightning-rod agent." And so the list went on, growing redder and redder, and more and more heartbreaking. Sixty persons had been killed, and two hundred and forty wounded. All the accounts bore just testimony to the activity and devotion of the detectives, and all closed with the remark that "three hundred thousand citizens and four detectives saw the dread creature, and two of the latter he destroyed."

I dreaded to hear the telegraphic instrument begin to click again. By and by the messages began to pour in, but I was happily disappointed in their nature. It was soon apparent that all trace of the elephant was lost. The fog had enabled him to search out a good hiding-place unobserved. Telegrams from the most absurdly distant points reported that a dim vast mass had been glimpsed there through the fog at such and such an hour, and was "undoubtedly the elephant." This dim vast mass had been glimpsed in New Haven, in New Jersey, in Pennsylvania, in interior New York, in Brooklyn, and even in the city of New York itself! But in all cases the dim vast mass had vanished quickly and left no trace. Every detective of the large force scattered over this huge extent of country sent his hourly report, and each and every one of them had a clue, and was shadowing something, and was hot upon the heels of it.

But the day passed without other result.

The next day the same.

The next just the same.

The newspaper reports began to grow monotonous with facts that amounted to nothing, clues which led to nothing, and theories which had nearly exhausted the elements which surprise and delight and dazzle.

By advice of the inspector I doubled the reward.

Four more dull days followed. Then came a bitter blow to the poor, hard-working detectives—the journalists declined to print their theories, and coldly said, "Give us a rest."

Two weeks after the elephant's disappearance I raised the reward to seventy-five thousand dollars by the inspector's advice. It was a great sum, but I felt that I would rather sacrifice my whole private fortune than lose my credit with my government. Now that the detectives were in adversity, the newspapers turned upon them, and began to fling the most stinging sarcasms at them. This gave the minstrels an idea, and they dressed themselves as detectives and hunted the elephant on the stage in the most extravagant way. The caricaturists made pictures of detectives scanning the country with spyglasses, while the elephant, at their backs, stole apples out of their pockets. And they made all sorts of ridiculous pictures of the detective badge—you have seen that badge printed in gold on the back of detective novels, no doubt—it is a wide-staring eye, with the legend, "WE NEVER SLEEP." When detectives called for a drink, the would-be facetious barkeeper resurrected an obsolete form of expression and said, "Will you have an eye-opener?" All the air was thick with sarcasms.

But there was one man who moved calm, untouched, unaffected, through it all. It was that heart of oak, the chief inspector. His brave eye never dropped, his serene confidence never wavered. He always said:

"Let them rail on; he laughs best who laughs last."

My admiration for the man grew into a species of worship. I was at his side always. His office had become an unpleasant place to me, and now became daily more and more so. Yet if he could endure it I meant to do so also—at least, as long as I could. So I came regularly, and stayed—the only outsider who seemed to be capable of it. Everybody wondered how I could; and often it seemed to me that I must desert, but at such times I looked into that calm and apparently unconscious face, and held my ground.

About three weeks after the elephant's disappearance I was about to say, one morning, that I should *have* to strike my colors and retire, when the great detective arrested the thought by proposing one more superb and masterly move.

This was to compromise with the robbers. The fertility of this man's invention exceeded anything I have ever seen, and I have had a wide intercourse with the world's finest minds. He said he was confident he could compromise for one hundred thousand dollars and recover the elephant. I said I believed I could scrape the amount together, but what would become of the poor detectives who had worked so faithfully? He said:

"In compromises they always get half."

This removed my only objection. So the inspector wrote two notes, in this form:

> DEAR MADAME—YOUR HUSBAND CAN MAKE A LARGE SUM OF MONEY (AND BE ENTIRELY PROTECTED FROM THE LAW) BY MAKING AN IMMEDIATE APPOINTMENT WITH ME.
>
> CHIEF BLUNT

He sent one of these by his confidential messenger to the "reputed wife" of Brick Duffy, and the other to the reputed wife of Red McFadden.

Within the hour these offensive answers came:

> YE OWLD FOOL: BRICK DUFFYS BIN DED 2 YERE.
>
> BRIDGET MAHONEY

CHIEF BAT—RED MCFADDEN IS HUNG AND IN HEVING 18 MONTH. ANY ASS BUT A DETECTIVE KNOSE THAT.

MARY O'HOOLIGAN

"I had long suspected these facts," said the inspector; "this testimony proves the unerring accuracy of my instinct."

The moment one resource failed him he was ready with another. He immediately wrote an advertisement for the morning papers, and I kept a copy of it:

A.—xwblv. 242 N. Tjnd—fz328wmlg. Ozpo,—; 2 m! ogw. Mum.

He said that if the thief was alive this would bring him to the usual rendezvous. He further explained that the usual rendezvous was a place where all business affairs between detectives and criminals were conducted. This meeting would take place at twelve the next night.

We could do nothing till then, and I lost no time in getting out of the office, and was grateful indeed for the privilege.

At eleven the next night I brought one hundred thousand dollars in bank-notes and put them into the chief's hands, and shortly afterward he took his leave, with the brave old undimmed confidence in his eye. An almost intolerable hour dragged to a close; then I heard his welcome tread, and rose gasping and tottered to meet him. How his fine eyes flamed with triumph! He said:

"We've compromised! The jokers will sing a different tune to-morrow! Follow me!"

He took a lighted candle and strode down into the vast vaulted basement where sixty detectives always slept, and where a score were now playing cards to while the time. I followed close after him. He walked swiftly down to the dim and remote end of the place, and just as I succumbed to the pangs of suffocation and was swooning away he stumbled and fell over the outlying members of a mighty object, and I heard him exclaim as he went down:

"Our noble profession is vindicated. Here is your elephant!"

I was carried to the office above and restored with carbolic acid. The whole detective force swarmed in, and such another season of triumphant rejoicing ensued as I had never witnessed before. The reporters were called, baskets of champagne were opened, toasts were drunk, the handshakings and congratulations were continuous and enthusiastic. Naturally the chief was the hero of the hour, and his happiness was so complete and had been so patiently and worthily and bravely won that it made me happy to see it, though I stood there a homeless beggar, my priceless charge dead, and my position in my country's service lost to me through what would always seem my fatally careless execution of a great trust. Many an eloquent eye testified its deep admiration for the chief, and many a detective's voice murmured, "Look at him—just the king of the profession; only give him a clue, it's all he wants, and there ain't anything hid that he can't find." The dividing of the fifty thousand dollars made great pleasure; when it was finished the chief made a little speech while he put his share in his pocket, in which he said, "Enjoy it, boys, for you've earned it; and, more than that, you've earned for the detective profession undying fame."

A telegram arrived, which read:

MONROE, MICH., 10 P.M.

FIRST TIME I'VE STRUCK A TELEGRAPH OFFICE IN OVER THREE WEEKS. HAVE FOLLOWED THOSE FOOTPRINTS, HORSEBACK, THROUGH THE WOODS, A THOUSAND

MILES TO HERE, AND THEY GET STRONGER AND BIGGER AND FRESHER EVERY DAY. DON'T WORRY—INSIDE OF ANOTHER WEEK I'LL HAVE THE ELEPHANT. THIS IS DEAD SURE.

DARLEY, DETECTIVE

The chief ordered three cheers for "Darley, one of the finest minds on the force," and then commanded that he be telegraphed to come home and receive his share of the reward.

So ended that marvelous episode of the stolen elephant. The newspapers were pleasant with praises once more, the next day, with one contemptible exception. This sheet said, "Great is the detective! He may be a little slow in finding a little thing like a mislaid elephant—he may hunt him all day and sleep with his rotting carcass all night for three weeks, but he will find him at last—if he can get the man who mislaid him to show him the place!"

Poor Hassan was lost to me forever. The cannon-shots had wounded him fatally, he had crept to that unfriendly place in the fog, and there, surrounded by his enemies and in constant danger of detection, he had wasted away with hunger and suffering till death gave him peace.

The compromise cost me one hundred thousand dollars; my detective expenses were forty-two thousand dollars more; I never applied for a place again under my government; I am a ruined man and a wanderer on the earth—but my admiration for that man, whom I believe to be the greatest detective the world has ever produced, remains undimmed to this day, and will so remain unto the end.

1882

The Invalid's Story

I SEEM SIXTY and married, but these effects are due to my condition and sufferings, for I am a bachelor, and only forty-one. It will be hard for you to believe that I, who am now but a shadow, was a hale, hearty man two short years ago—a man of iron, a very athlete!—yet such is the simple truth. But stranger still than this fact is the way in which I lost my health. I lost it through helping to take care of a box of guns on a two-hundred-mile railway journey one winter's night. It is the actual truth, and I will tell you about it.

I belong in Cleveland, Ohio. One winter's night, two years ago, I reached home just after dark, in a driving snow-storm, and the first thing I heard when I entered the house was that my dearest boyhood friend and schoolmate, John B. Hackett, had died the day before, and that his last utterance had been a desire that I would take his remains home to his poor old father and mother in Wisconsin. I was greatly shocked and grieved, but there was no time to waste in emotions; I must start at once. I took the card, marked "Deacon Levi Hackett, Bethlehem, Wisconsin," and hurried off through the whistling storm to the railway-station. Arrived there I found the long white-pine box which had been described to me; I fastened the card to it with some tacks, saw it put safely aboard the express-car, and then ran into the eating-room to provide myself with a sandwich and some cigars. When I returned, presently, there was my coffin-box *back again*, apparently, and a young fellow examining around it, with a card in his hands, and some tacks and a hammer! I was astonished and puzzled. He began to nail on his card, and I rushed out to the express-car, in a good deal of a state of mind, to ask for an explanation. But no—there was my box, all right, in the express-car; it hadn't been disturbed. [The fact is that without my suspecting it a prodigious mistake had been made. I was carrying off a box of *guns* which that young fellow had come to the station to ship to a rifle company in Peoria, Illinois, and *he* had got my corpse!] Just then the conductor sang out "All aboard," and I jumped into the express-car and got a comfortable seat on a bale of buckets. The expressman was there, hard at work—a plain man of fifty, with a simple, honest, good-natured face, and a breezy, practical heartiness in his general style. As the train moved off a stranger skipped into the car and set a package of peculiarly mature and capable Limburger cheese on one end of my coffin-box—I mean my box of guns. That is to say, I know *now* that it was Limburger cheese, but at that time I never had heard of the article in my life, and of course was wholly ignorant of its character. Well, we sped through the wild night, the bitter storm raged on, a cheerless misery stole over me, my heart went down, down, down! The old expressman made a brisk remark or two about the tempest and the arctic weather, slammed his sliding doors to, and bolted them, closed his window down tight, and then went bustling around, here and there and yonder, setting things to rights, and all the time contentedly humming "Sweet By and By," in a low tone, and flatting a good deal. Presently I began to detect a most evil and searching odor stealing about on the frozen air. This depressed my spirits still more, because of course I attributed it to my poor departed friend. There was something infinitely saddening about his calling himself to my remembrance in this dumb, pathetic way, so it was hard to keep the tears back. Moreover, it distressed me on account of the old expressman, who, I was afraid, might notice it. However, he went humming tranquilly on, and gave no sign; and for this I was grateful. Grateful, yes, but still uneasy; and soon I began to feel more and more uneasy every minute, for every minute that went by that odor thickened up the more, and got to be more and more gamy and hard to stand. Presently, having got things arranged to his satisfaction, the expressman got some wood and made up a tremendous fire in his stove. This distressed me more than I can tell, for I could not but feel that it was a mistake. I was sure that the effect would be deleterious upon my poor departed friend. Thompson—the expressman's name was Thompson, as I found out in the course of the night—now went poking around his car, stopping up whatever stray cracks he could find, remarking that it didn't make any difference what kind of a night it was outside, he calculated to make *us* comfortable, anyway. I said nothing, but I believed he was not choosing the right way. Meantime he was humming to himself just as before; and meantime, too, the stove was getting hotter and hotter, and the place closer and closer. I felt myself growing pale and qualmish, but grieved in silence and said nothing. Soon I noticed that the "Sweet By and By" was gradually fading out; next it ceased altogether, and there was an ominous stillness. After a few moments Thompson said—

"Pfew! I reckon it ain't no cinnamon 't I've loaded up thish-yer stove with!"

He gasped once or twice, then moved toward the cof—gun-box, stood over that Limburger cheese part of a moment, then came back and sat down near me, looking a good deal impressed. After a contemplative pause, he said, indicating the box with a gesture—

"Friend of yourn?"

"Yes," I said with a sigh.

"He's pretty ripe, *ain't* he!"

Nothing further was said for perhaps a couple of minutes, each being busy with his own thoughts; then Thompson said, in a low, awed voice—

"Sometimes it's uncertain whether they're really gone or not—*seem* gone, you know—body warm, joints limber—and so, although you *think* they're gone, you don't really know. I've had cases in my car. It's perfectly awful, becuz *you* don't know what minute they'll rise up and look at you!" Then, after a pause, and slightly lifting his elbow toward the box,—"But *he* ain't in no trance! No, sir, I go bail for *him!*"

We sat some time, in meditative silence, listening to the wind and the roar of the train; then Thompson said, with a good deal of feeling:

"Well-a-well, we've all got to go, they ain't no getting around it. Man that is born of woman is of few days and far between, as Scriptur' says. Yes, you look at it any way you want to, it's awful solemn and cur'us: they ain't *nobody* can get around it; *all's* got to go—just *everybody*, as you may say. One day you're hearty and strong"—here he scrambled to his feet and broke a pane and stretched his nose out at it a moment or two, then sat down again while I struggled up and thrust my nose out at the same place, and this we kept on doing every now and then—"and next day he's cut down like the grass, and the places which knowed him then knows him no more forever, as Scriptur' says. Yes'ndeedy, it's awful solemn and cur'us; but we've all got to go, one time or another; they ain't no getting around it."

There was another long pause; then—

"What did he die of?"

I said I didn't know.

"How long has he been dead?"

It seemed judicious to enlarge the facts to fit the probabilities; so I said:

"Two or three days."

But it did no good; for Thompson received it with an injured look which plainly said, "Two or three *years*, you mean." Then he went right along, placidly ignoring my statement, and gave his views at considerable length upon the un-wisdom of putting off burials too long. Then he lounged off toward the box, stood a moment, then came back on a sharp trot and visited the broken pane, observing:

"'Twould 'a' ben a dum sight better, all around, if they'd started him along last summer."

Thompson sat down and buried his face in his red silk handkerchief, and began to slowly sway and rock his body like one who is doing his best to endure the almost unendurable. By this time the fragrance—if you may call it fragrance—was just about suffocating, as near as you can come at it. Thompson's face was turning gray; I knew mine hadn't any color left in it. By and by Thompson rested his forehead in his left hand, with his elbow on his knee, and sort of waved his red handkerchief toward the box with his other hand, and said:

"I've carried a many a one of 'em—some of 'em considerable overdue, too—but, lordy, he just lays over 'em all!—and does it *easy*. Cap, they was heliotrope to *him!*"

This recognition of my poor friend gratified me, in spite of the sad circumstances, because it had so much the sound of a compliment.

Pretty soon it was plain that something had got to be done. I suggested cigars. Thompson thought it was a good idea. He said:

"Likely it'll modify him some."

We puffed gingerly along for a while, and tried hard to imagine that things were improved. But it wasn't any use. Before very long, and without any consultation, both cigars were quietly dropped from our nerveless fingers at the same moment.

Thompson said, with a sigh:

"No, Cap, it don't modify him worth a cent. Fact is, it makes him worse, becuz it appears to stir up his ambition. What do you reckon we better do, now?"

I was not able to suggest anything; indeed, I had to be swallowing and swallowing all the time, and did not like to trust myself to speak. Thompson fell to maundering, in a desultory and low-spirited way, about the miserable experiences of this night; and he got to referring to my poor friend by various titles—sometimes military ones, sometimes civil ones; and I noticed that as fast as my poor friend's effectiveness grew, Thompson promoted him accordingly—gave him a bigger title. Finally he said:

"I've got an idea. Suppos'n' we buckle down to it and give the Colonel a bit of a shove toward t'other end of the car?—about ten foot, say. He wouldn't have so much influence, then, don't you reckon?"

I said it was a good scheme. So we took in a good fresh breath at the broken pane, calculating to hold it till we got through; then we went there and bent over that deadly cheese and took a grip on the box. Thompson nodded "All ready," and then we threw ourselves forward with all our might; but Thompson slipped, and slumped down with his nose on the cheese, and his breath got loose. He gagged and gasped, and floundered up and made a break for the door, pawing the air and saying hoarsely, "Don't hender me!—gimme the road! I'm a-dying; gimme the road!" Out on the cold platform I sat down and held his head awhile, and he revived. Presently he said:

"Do you reckon we started the Gen'rul any?"

I said no; we hadn't budged him.

"Well, then, *that* idea's up the flume. We got to think up something else. He's suited wher' he is, I reckon; and if that's the way he feels about it, and has made up his mind that he don't wish to be disturbed, you bet he's a-going to have his own way in the business. Yes, better leave him right wher' he is, long as he wants it so; becuz he holds all the trumps, don't you know, and so it stands to reason that the man that lays out to alter his plans for him is going to get left."

But we couldn't stay out there in that mad storm; we should have frozen to death. So we went in again and shut the door, and began to suffer once more and take turns at the break in the window. By and by, as we were starting away from a station where we had stopped a moment Thompson pranced in cheerily, and exclaimed:

"We're all right, now! I reckon we've got the Commodore this time. I judge I've got the stuff here that'll take the tuck out of him."

It was carbolic acid. He had a carboy of it. He sprinkled it all around everywhere; in fact he drenched everything with it, rifle-box, cheese and all. Then we sat down, feeling pretty hopeful. But it wasn't for long. You see the two perfumes began to mix, and then—well, pretty soon we made a break for the door; and out there Thompson swabbed his face with his bandanna and said in a kind of disheartened way:

"It ain't no use. We can't buck agin *him*. He just utilizes everything we put up to modify him with, and gives it his own flavor and plays it back on us. Why, Cap, don't you know, it's as much as a hundred times worse in there now than it was when he first got a-going. I never *did* see one of 'em warm up to his work so, and take such a dumnation interest in it. No, sir, I never did, as long as I've ben on the road; and I've carried a many a one of 'em, as I was telling you."

We went in again after we were frozen pretty stiff; but my, we couldn't *stay* in, now. So we just waltzed back and forth, freezing, and thawing, and stifling, by turns. In about an hour we stopped at another station; and as we left it Thompson came in with a bag, and said—

"Cap, I'm a-going to chance him once more—just this once; and if we don't fetch him this time, the thing for us to do, is to just throw up the sponge and withdraw from the canvass. That's the way *I* put it up."

He had brought a lot of chicken feathers, and dried apples, and leaf tobacco, and rags, and old shoes, and sulphur, and asafetida, and one thing or another; and he piled them on a breadth of sheet iron in the middle of the floor, and set fire to them.

When they got well started, I couldn't see, myself, how even the corpse could stand it. All that went before was just simply poetry to that smell—but mind you, the original smell stood up out of it just as sublime as ever—fact is, these other smells just seemed to give it a better hold; and my, how rich it was! I didn't make these reflections there—there wasn't time—made them on the platform. And breaking for the platform, Thompson got suffocated and fell; and before I got him dragged out, which I did by the collar, I was mighty near gone myself. When we revived, Thompson said dejectedly:

"We got to stay out here, Cap. We got to do it. They ain't no other way. The Governor wants to travel alone, and he's fixed so he can out-vote us."

And presently he added:

"And don't you know, we're *pisoned*. It's *our* last trip, you can make up your mind to it. Typhoid fever is what's going to come of this. I feel it a-coming right now. Yes, sir, we're elected, just as sure as you're born."

We were taken from the platform an hour later, frozen and insensible, at the next station, and I went straight off into a virulent fever, and never knew anything again for three weeks. I found out, then, that I had spent that awful night with a harmless box of rifles and a lot of innocent cheese; but the news was too late to save *me*; imagination had done its work, and my health was permanently shattered; neither Bermuda nor any other land can ever bring it back to me. This is my last trip; I am on my way home to die.

1882

Luck*

It was at a banquet in London in honor of one of the two or three conspicuously illustrious English military names of this generation. For reasons which will presently appear, I will withhold his real name and titles and call him Lieutenant-General Lord Arthur Scoresby, Y.C., K.C.B., etc., etc., etc. What a fascination there is in a renowned name! There sat the man, in actual flesh, whom I had heard of so many thousands of times since that day, thirty years before, when his name shot suddenly to the zenith from a Crimean battlefield, to remain forever celebrated. It was food and drink to me to look, and look, and look at that demi-god; scanning, searching, noting: the quietness, the reserve, the noble gravity of his countenance; the simple honesty that expressed itself all over him; the sweet unconsciousness of his greatness—unconsciousness of the hundreds of admiring eyes fastened upon him, unconsciousness of the deep, loving, sincere worship welling out of the breasts of those people and flowing toward him.

The clergyman at my left was an old acquaintance of mine—clergyman now, but had spent the first half of his life in the camp and field and as an instructor in the military school at Woolwich. Just at the moment I have been talking about a veiled and singular light glimmered in his eyes and he leaned down and muttered confidentially to me—indicating the hero of the

---

* This is not a fancy sketch. I got it from a clergyman who was an instructor at Woolwich forty years ago, and who vouched for its truth. M.T.

banquet with a gesture:

"Privately—he's an absolute fool."

This verdict was a great surprise to me. If its subject had been Napoleon, or Socrates, or Solomon, my astonishment could not have been greater. Two things I was well aware of: that the Reverend was a man of strict veracity and that his judgment of men was good. Therefore I knew, beyond doubt or question, that the world was mistaken about this hero: he *was* a fool. So I meant to find out, at a convenient moment, how the Reverend, all solitary and alone, had discovered the secret.

Some days later the opportunity came, and this is what the Reverend told me:

About forty years ago I was an instructor in the military academy at Woolwich. I was present in one of the sections when young Scoresby underwent his preliminary examination. I was touched to the quick with pity, for the rest of the class answered up brightly and handsomely, while he—why, dear me, he didn't know *anything,* so to speak. He was evidently good, and sweet, and lovable, and guileless; and so it was exceedingly painful to see him stand there, as serene as a graven image, and deliver himself of answers which were veritably miraculous for stupidity and ignorance. All the compassion in me was aroused in his behalf. I said to myself, when he comes to be examined again he will be flung over, of course; so it will be simply a harmless act of charity to ease his fall as much as I can. I took him aside and found that he knew a little of Cæsar's history; and as he didn't know anything else, I went to work and drilled him like a galley-slave on a certain line of stock questions concerning Cæsar which I knew would be used. If you'll believe me, he went through with flying colors on examination day! He went through on that purely superficial "cram," and got compliments too, while others, who knew a thousand times more than he, got plucked. By some strangely lucky accident—an accident not likely to happen twice in a century—he was asked no question outside of the narrow limits of his drill.

It was stupefying. Well, all through his course I stood by him, with something of the sentiment which a mother feels for a crippled child; and he always saved himself—just by miracle, apparently.

Now, of course, the thing that would expose him and kill him at last was mathematics. I resolved to make his death as easy as I could; so I drilled him and crammed him, and crammed him and drilled him, just on the line of questions which the examiners would be most likely to use, and then launched him on his fate. Well, sir, try to conceive of the result: to my consternation, he took the first prize! And with it he got a perfect ovation in the way of compliments.

Sleep? There was no more sleep for me for a week. My conscience tortured me day and night. What I had done I had done purely through charity, and only to ease the poor youth's fall. I never had dreamed of any such preposterous results as the thing that had happened. I felt as guilty and miserable as Frankenstein. Here was a wooden-head whom I had put in the way of glittering promotions and prodigious responsibilities, and but one thing could happen: he and his responsibilities would all go to ruin together at the first opportunity.

The Crimean War had just broken out. Of course there had to be a war, I said to myself. We couldn't have peace and give this donkey a chance to die before he is found out. I waited for the earthquake. It came. And it made me reel when it did come. He was actually gazetted to a captaincy in a marching regiment! Better men grow old and gray in the service before they climb to a sublimity like that. And who could ever have foreseen that they would go and put such a load of responsibility on such green and inadequate shoulders? I could just barely have stood it if they had made him a cornet; but a captain—think of it! I thought my hair would turn white.

Consider what I did—I who so loved repose and inaction. I said to myself, I am responsible to the country for this, and I must go along with him and protect the country against him as far as I can. So I took my poor little capital that I had saved up through years of work and grinding economy, and went with a sigh and bought a cornetcy in his regiment, and away we went to the field.

And there—oh, dear, it was awful. Blunders?—why he never did anything *but* blunder. But, you see, nobody was in the fellow's secret. Everybody had him focused wrong, and necessarily misinterpreted his performance every time. Consequently they took his idiotic blunders for inspirations of genius. They did, honestly! His mildest blunders were enough to make a man in his right mind cry; and they did make me cry—and rage and rave, too, privately. And the thing that kept me always in a sweat of apprehension was the fact that every fresh blunder he made increased the luster of his reputation! I kept saying to myself, he'll get so high that when discovery does finally come it will be like the sun falling out of the sky.

He went right along, up from grade to grade, over the dead bodies of his superiors, until at last, in the hottest moment of the battle of —— down went our colonel, and my heart jumped into my mouth, for Scoresby was next in rank! Now for it, said I; we'll all land in Sheol in ten minutes, sure.

The battle was awfully hot; the allies were steadily giving way all over the field. Our regiment occupied a position that was vital; a blunder now must be destruction. At this crucial moment, what does this immortal fool do but detach the regiment from its place and order a charge over a neighboring hill where there wasn't a suggestion of an enemy! "There you go!" I said to myself; "this *is* the end at last."

And away we did go, and were over the shoulder of the hill before the insane movement could be discovered and stopped. And what did we find? An entire and unsuspected Russian army in reserve! And what happened? We were eaten up? That is necessarily what would have happened in ninety-nine cases out of a hundred. But no; those Russians argued that no single regiment would come browsing around there at such a time. It must be the entire English army, and that the sly Russian game was detected and blocked; so they turned tail, and away they went, pell-mell, over the hill and down into the field, in wild confusion, and we after them; they themselves broke the solid Russian center in the field, and tore through, and in no time there was the most tremendous rout you ever saw, and the defeat of the allies was turned into a sweeping and splendid victory! Marshal Canrobert looked on, dizzy with astonishment, admiration, and delight; and sent right off for Scoresby, and hugged him, and decorated him on the field in presence of all the armies!

And what was Scoresby's blunder that time? Merely the mistaking his right hand for his left—that was all. An order had come to him to fall back and support our right; and, instead, he fell *forward* and went over the hill to the left. But the name he won that day as a marvelous military genius filled the world with his glory, and that glory will never fade while history books last.

He is just as good and sweet and lovable and unpretending as a man can be, but he doesn't know enough to come in when it rains. Now that is absolutely true. He is the supremest ass in the universe; and until half an hour ago nobody knew it but himself and me. He has been pursued, day by day and year by year, by a most phenomenal and astonishing luckiness. He has been a shining soldier in all our wars for a generation; he has littered his whole military life with blunders, and yet has never committed one that didn't make him a knight or a baronet or a lord or something. Look at his breast; why, he is just clothed in domestic and foreign decorations. Well, sir, every one of them is the record of some shouting stupidity or other; and, taken together, they are proof that the very best thing in all this world that can befall a man is to be born lucky. I say again, as I said at the banquet, Scoresby's an absolute fool.

1891

Hunting the Deceitful Turkey

When I was a boy my uncle and his big boys hunted with the rifle, the youngest boy Fred and I with a shotgun—a small single-barrelled shotgun which was properly suited to our size and strength; it was not much heavier than a broom. We carried it turn about, half an hour at a time. I was not able to hit anything with it, but I liked to try. Fred and I hunted feathered small game, the others hunted deer, squirrels, wild turkeys, and such things. My uncle and the big boys were good shots. They killed hawks and wild geese and such like on the wing; and they didn't wound or kill squirrels, they *stunned* them. When the dogs treed a squirrel, the squirrel would scamper aloft and run out on a limb and flatten himself along it, hoping to make himself invisible in that way—and not quite succeeding. You could see his wee little ears sticking up. You couldn't see his nose, but you knew where it was. Then the hunter, despising a "rest" for his rifle, stood up and took offhand aim at the limb and sent a bullet into it immediately under the squirrel's nose, and down tumbled the animal, unwounded but unconscious; the dogs gave him a shake and he was dead. Sometimes when the distance was great and the wind not accurately allowed for, the bullet would hit the squirrel's head; the dogs could do as they pleased with that one—the hunter's pride was hurt, and he wouldn't allow it to go into the gamebag.

In the first faint gray of the dawn the stately wild turkeys would be stalking around in great flocks, and ready to be sociable and answer invitations to come and converse with other excursionists of their kind. The hunter concealed himself and imitated the turkey-call by sucking the air through the legbone of a turkey which had previously answered a call like that and lived only just long enough to regret it. There is nothing that furnishes a perfect turkey-call except that bone. Another of Nature's treacheries, you see. She is full of them; half the time she doesn't know which she likes best—to betray her child or protect it. In the case of the turkey she is badly mixed: she gives it a bone to be used in getting it into trouble, and she also furnishes it with a trick for getting itself out of the trouble again. When a mamma-turkey answers an invitation and finds she has made a mistake in accepting it, she does as the mamma-partridge does—remembers a previous engagement and goes limping and scrambling away, pretending to be very lame; and at the same time she is saying to her not-visible children, "Lie low, keep still, don't expose yourselves; I shall be back as soon as I have beguiled this shabby swindler out of the country."

When a person is ignorant and confiding, this immoral device can have tiresome results. I followed an ostensibly lame turkey over a considerable part of the United States one morning, because I believed in her and could not think she would deceive a mere boy, and one who was trusting her and considering her honest. I had the single-barrelled shotgun, but my idea was to catch her alive. I often got within rushing distance of her, and then made my rush; but always, just as I made my final plunge and put my hand down where her back had been, it wasn't there; it was only two or three inches from there and I brushed the tail-feathers as I landed on my stomach—a very close call, but still not quite close enough; that is, not close enough for success, but just close enough to convince me that I could do it next time. She always waited for me, a little piece away, and let on to be resting and greatly fatigued; which was a lie, but I believed it, for I still thought her honest long after I ought to have begun to doubt her, suspecting that this was no way for a high-minded bird to be acting. I followed, and followed, and followed, making my periodical rushes, and getting up and brushing the dust off, and resuming the voyage with patient confidence; indeed, with a confidence which grew, for I could see by the change of climate and vegetation that we were getting up into the high latitudes, and as she always looked a little tireder and a little more discouraged after each rush, I judged that I was safe to win, in the end, the competition being purely a matter of staying power and the advantage lying with me from the start because she was lame.

Along in the afternoon I began to feel fatigued myself. Neither of us had had any rest since we first started on the excursion, which was upwards of ten hours before, though latterly we had paused awhile after rushes, I letting on to be thinking about something else; but neither of us sincere, and both of us waiting for the other to call game but in no real hurry about it, for indeed those little evanescent snatches of rest were very grateful to the feelings of us both; it would naturally be so, skirmishing along like that ever since dawn and not a bite in the meantime; at least for me, though sometimes as she lay on her side fanning herself with a wing and praying for strength to get out of this difficulty a grasshopper happened along whose time had come, and that was well for her, and fortunate, but I had nothing—nothing the whole day.

More than once, after I was very tired, I gave up taking her alive, and was going to shoot her, but I never did it, although it was my right, for I did not believe I could hit her; and besides, she always stopped and posed, when I raised the gun, and this made me suspicious that she knew about me and my marksmanship, and so I did not care to expose myself to remarks.

I did not get her, at all. When she got tired of the game at last, she rose from almost under my hand and flew aloft with the rush and whir of a shell and lit on the highest limb of a great tree and sat down and crossed her legs and smiled down at me, and seemed gratified to see me so astonished.

I was ashamed, and also lost; and it was while wandering the woods hunting for myself that I found a deserted log cabin and had one of the best meals there that in my life-days I have eaten. The weed-grown garden was full of ripe tomatoes, and I ate them ravenously, though I had never liked them before. Not more than two or three times since have I tasted anything that was so delicious as those tomatoes. I surfeited myself with them, and did not taste another one until I was in middle life. I can eat them now, but I do not like the look of them. I suppose we have all experienced a surfeit at one time or another. Once, in stress of circumstances, I ate part of a barrel of sardines, there being nothing else at hand, but since then I have always been able to get along without sardines.

1906

Biographical Timeline

1823 Virginia native John Marshall Clemens (1798–1847) marries Jane Lampton (1803–1890), a native of Kentucky, on May 6.

The couple moves to Fentress County, Tennessee, where John Clemens practices law, operates a general store, and serves as a county commissioner, county clerk, and attorney general.

1832 John Clemens serves as postmaster in Pall Mall, a small unincorporated community in Fentress County, Tennessee. Over time he speculates unsuccessfully in land and opens four stores that are unprofitable.

1835 Clemens family moves to Florida, Missouri. Samuel Langhorne Clemens (SLC) is born two months prematurely on November 30, 1835, the sixth of seven children. Halley's Comet, a short-period comet visible from Earth every seventy-five to seventy-six years, is in the skies. Halley is the only known short-period comet that is regularly visible to the naked eye from Earth, and thus the only naked-eye comet that can appear twice in a human lifetime.

1839 Clemens family moves to Hannibal, Missouri. Judge Clemens operates a general store. He eventually serves as a steamboat and railroad commissioner and becomes a county judge.

1843	Family moves into house later known as SLC's boyhood home.
1846	Due to poverty, Clemens family moves in with Grant family above Grant's Drug Store.
1847	Judge Clemens dies of pleurisy and pneumonia on March 24. Family moves back to boyhood home.
1848	SLC's formal education ends; he becomes a printer's apprentice to Joseph Ament of the *Missouri Courier* newspaper.
1850	Elder brother Orion (1825–1897) returns to Hannibal in September and purchases the *Western Union,* a local newspaper.
1851	SLC begins working as a typesetter, contributing articles and humorous sketches to the *Hannibal Journal*, which Orion by then owns.
1852	SLC edits Orion's newspaper while Orion is away. SLC submits two sketches to *The Saturday Evening Post.* His sketch "The Dandy Frightening the Squatter" is published in the May 1 issue of *Carpet-Bag* of Boston, Massachusetts.
1853	SLC leaves Hannibal in June to become a journeyman printer in New York City, Philadelphia, St. Louis, and Cincinnati; joins the newly formed International Typographical Union, the printers trade union.
	Orion moves their mother, Jane Clemens, and Henry Clemens to Iowa.
1854	SLC visits Washington, D.C., in February. Spends summer in Muscatine, Iowa, and works with brother Orion, who runs the *Muscatine Journal.*

1855 Spends winter and spring in St. Louis.

1856 Works as assistant in job at a printing shop in Cincinnati, Ohio. Goes to work for Orion at *Orion's Daily Post,* located in Keokuk, Iowa, until fall of 1856.

1857 Becomes apprentice Mississippi River steamboat pilot under Captain Horace Bixby of the *Paul Jones.*

1858 While training to become a pilot, persuades his younger brother Henry to work with him; arranges a post of mud clerk for Henry on the steamboat *Pennsylvania.* On June 13, the steamboat's boiler explodes; Henry succumbs to his wounds on June 21. SLC is guilt-ridden and holds himself responsible for the rest of his life.

1859 On April 9 becomes fully licensed pilot. Serves on the steamer *A. B. Chambers* with Grant Marsh, who becomes famous for his exploits as a steamboat captain on the Missouri River.

1861 The outbreak of Civil War curtails traffic along the Mississippi River, ending SLC's piloting career.

Enlists briefly in a local Confederate unit; serves for only two weeks.

Travels by stage coach to Carson City, Nevada, with brother Orion, who had been appointed Secretary to the Territorial Governor of Nevada, James Nye.

1862 After failing as a miner on the Comstock Lode, becomes a reporter for the Virginia City *Territorial Enterprise.*

1863 First uses pen name Mark Twain on piece for the Virginia City *Territorial Enterprise.*

1864 Leaves for California in May to begin work at the *San Francisco Call* newspaper.

1865 Tries his hand at gold mining at Angels Camp, California, where he hears the Jumping Frog story. "Jim Smiley and His Jumping Frog" is published in the November 18 issue of *The New York Saturday Press.*

1866 Travels to Sandwich Islands (Hawaii) as correspondent for *The Sacramento Union.* Returns and lectures about his experiences.

1867 *The Celebrated Jumping Frog of Calaveras County and Other Sketches,* SLC's first collection of short stories, is published.

Visits New York via Nicaragua.

Makes Midwest lecture tour that includes stops in St. Louis, Hannibal, Quincy, and Keokuk.

Travels to Europe and the Middle East as a correspondent for *The San Francisco Alta California.* On this trip meets Charles Langdon, who shows him a picture of his sister Olivia. Twain later claims to have fallen in love at first sight. Briefly serves as secretary to Senator William Stewart of Nevada in Washington, D.C.

1868 SLC is offered honorary membership in Yale University's secret society Scroll and Key.

Signs contract for his first book, *The Innocents Abroad.*

Travels to California to obtain the release of some of his letters published in newspapers there. Conducts a Midwest lecture tour in November and December.

1869 *The Innocents Abroad* (travel narrative).

Becomes engaged to Olivia Louise Langdon of Elmira, New York, on February 4.

In August, buys a stake in the *Buffalo Express* newspaper and starts work as a writer and editor.

1870 Marries Olivia Langdon in Elmira on February 2 and settles in Buffalo.

Son, Langdon, is born on November 7.

Through Olivia and her family, meets abolitionists, socialists, principled atheists, and activists for women's rights and social equality, including Harriet Beecher Stowe, Frederick Douglass, and utopian socialist writer William Dean Howells, who becomes a lifelong friend.

1871 *Mark Twain's (Burlesque) Autobiography and First Romance* (story collection).

Visits London, England.

Sells *Buffalo Express* interest and moves to Hartford, Connecticut, in October.

Receives U.S. patent for adjustable garment strap (to replace suspenders).

1872 *Roughing It* (travel narrative).

Daughter Susan "Susy" is born on March 19.

Son Langdon dies of diphtheria in June.

1873 *The Gilded Age*, written with Charles Dudley Warner (novel).

SLC begins building large house in Hartford, Connecticut, preserved today as Mark Twain House.

During the 1870s and 1880s, the family summers at Quarry Farm in Elmira, New York, the home of Olivia's sister, Susan Crane.

1873 *The Gilded Age* (novel).

Receives patent for self-pasting scrapbook, the only one of SLC's three inventions that makes money.

1874 Daughter Clara is born on June 8.

1875 *Sketches New and Old* (story collection).

1876 *The Adventures of Tom Sawyer* (novel); *Old Times on the Mississippi* (travel).

1877 *A True Story and the Recent Carnival of Crime* (story collection); *Some Rambling Notes of an Idle Excursion* (travel).

Speaks at John Greenleaf Whittier's seventieth birthday celebration.

1878–79 *Punch, Brothers, Punch! and Other Sketches* (story collection).

Travels with family to Europe: Heidelberg, Alps, Italy, Munich.

1880 *A Tramp Abroad* (travel).

Daughter Jean is born on July 26.

1881 *The Prince and the Pauper* (novel). SLC begins investing in the Paige typesetter.

1882 Makes trip up the Mississippi from New Orleans to Minnesota to gather information for *Life on the Mississippi.* Visits Hannibal.

1883 *Life on the Mississippi* (travel).

1884 *Adventures of Huckleberry Finn* (novel) published in England.

Conducts national lecture tour with George Washington Cable from November to February 1885.

1885 *Adventures of Huckleberry Finn* is published in the U.S. by SLC's own publishing company, Charles L. Webster & Company. SLC publishing house releases a bestseller, *The Personal Memoirs of Ulysses S. Grant,* a hugely successful autobiography.

1888 *Mark Twain's Library of Humor* (story collection).

Receives Master of Arts degree from Yale University.

1889 *A Connecticut Yankee in King Arthur's Court* (novel)

Meets Rudyard Kipling in Elmira, New York.

1890 Visits ailing mother in Keokuk, Iowa. Mother dies on October 27.

1891 Mark Twain's Memory Builder Game is put on the market, his third patent.

To ease financial pressures caused by Charles L. Webster & Company expenses and unprofitable type-setter investment, the Clemenses close the Hartford house and relocate to Europe, making extended stays in Germany, France, and Italy.

1892 *The American Claimant* (novel); *Merry Tales* (story collection).

1893 *The £1,000,000 Bank Note and Other New Stories* (story collection).

Speaking successes earn Twain title "Belle of New York," in the words of biographer Albert Bigelow Paine.

Begins friendship with Henry Huttleston Rogers, a principal of Standard Oil, who takes charge of the family's finances.

1894 *Pudd'nhead Wilson* (novel); *Tom Sawyer Abroad* (novel).

Charles L. Webster & Company, SLC's publishing firm, faces financial crisis following Panic of 1893; on the insistence of Henry Rogers, SLC files bankruptcy in April, then transfers the copyrights on his written works to his wife to prevent creditors from gaining possession of them. Henry Rogers oversees financial repayments of SLC's debts.

1895 The Paige typesetting machine, in which SLC invested $300,000 (the equivalent of $9,000,000 in 2022), is rendered obsolete by the Linotype. In order to pay debts, SLC embarks on round-the-world lecture tour that includes visits to Fiji, Australia, New Zealand, Sri Lanka, India, Mauritius, and South Africa.

1896 *Personal Recollections of Joan of Arc* (novel); *Tom Sawyer, Detective* (novel).

Daughter Susy dies of meningitis on August 18.

1897 *Following the Equator* (travel).

SLC and his family stay in Europe another four years, mainly in England and Austria.

1898 Completes repayment of all debts.

1900 Argues copyright law before House of Lords in England. After extended stays in Austria, Switzerland, Sweden, England, returns to America in October.

1901 *The Battle Hymn of the Republic, Updated* (lyric).

In January, begins serving as vice-president of the Anti-Imperialist League of New York.

Family summers at Lake Saranac in the Adirondacks. Receives honorary doctorate degree at Yale University.

1902 Aboard his friend Henry Rogers's yacht, *Kanawha,* visits Nova Scotia and the Caribbean.

Helps dedicate Eugene Field's House as a museum property in St. Louis prior to visiting Hannibal.

Makes final visit to Hannibal, Missouri, from May 29 to June 1. Hands out graduation diplomas to Hannibal High School graduating class.

Travels on to Columbia, Missouri, to receive honorary Doctorate Degree from University of Missouri.

1903 Because of Olivia Clemens's failing health, family relocates to Florence, Italy.

1904 *Extracts from Adam's Diary* (novella).

Olivia dies on June 5.

SLC returns to New York City.

1905 *King Leopold's Soliloquy* (satire).

Seventieth birthday dinner at Delmonico's in New York.

Biographer Albert Bigelow Paine begins to collect dictations for autobiography.

1906 *Eve's Diary* (novella); *The $30,000 Bequest and Other Stories* (story collection); material from *Chapters from My Autobiography* (autobiography); *What Is Man?* published anonymously.

SLC begins final, concentrated work on his autobiography.

1907 *A Horse's Tale* (novel); additional material from *Chapters from My Autobiography* (autobiography).

SLC travels to England to receive honorary Doctorate of Letters (D.Litt.) from Oxford University.

1908 SLC moves into his final home, Stormfield, in Redding, Connecticut, on June 18. Visitors include Helen Keller and Laura Hawkins Frazer (model for Becky Thatcher).

1909 *Is Shakespeare Dead?* (semi-autobiographical satire).

SLC says, "I came in with Halley's Comet in 1835. It is coming again next year, and I expect to go out with it. It will be the greatest disappointment of my life if I don't go out with Halley's Comet. The Almighty has said, no doubt: 'Now here are these two unaccountable freaks; they came in together, they must go out together.'"

Close friend Henry Rogers dies on May 20.

Daughter Clara marries Ossip Gabrilowitsch, a Russian concert pianist and conductor, at Stormfield, on October 6.

Daughter Jean dies on December 24.

1910 Makes last trip to Bermuda for health reasons. Heart complications set in; returns home to Stormfield.

Samuel Langhorne Clemens dies on April 21, 1910, the day after Halley's Comet made its closest approach to Earth.

SLC is buried in wife's family's plot, Woodlawn Cemetery, Elmira, New York.

1916 *The Mysterious Stranger* (novel, posthumously published).

www.ingramcontent.com/pod-product-compliance
Lightning Source LLC
Chambersburg PA
CBHW030558130626
46552CB00006B/2588
9781957240930